RED LIGHT LADIES

USA TODAY BESTSELLING AUTHOR

YOLANDA OLSON

BLURB

We roam the streets of Amsterdam looking to sell our bodies.

Hell, we'd sell our souls if we could, but those don't belong to us anymore.

They belong to the man who decided that we belong to him.

It's his house, his rules—*our* bodies.

Four of us aren't what we seem.

We look for ways to leave this place, for ways to be free.

But all freedom comes with a price, and some prices are far too high to pay.

Even for us.

ALL THAT

MATTERS

 BLURB

Who knew that a few nights of being unfaithful would lead to this?

I sure as hell didn't, and I don't know how to get out of this.

I used to be a beautiful, strong girl.

I used to be loved by a good man, successful in my own right, and adored by almost every stranger I met on the street.

I used to be a lot of things.

Some of them I miss, others I took for granted.

Now that it's too late to see the error of everything I ever did to the man that I loved, I know it's too late.

Tell me your pleasure.

Pay the right price.

I'll be yours for the night.

While this is never the life I wanted for myself, at least I know I'll be all of the things I used to be again.

Even if it's just for the night.

PROLOGUE

I USED to be Amity Crane.

I used to be successful, strong, beautiful, loved. I used to be the girl who would make guys pant when I walked by them, the girl that took the world by storm, and the girl that loved a good adventure more than anything else. I was the girl obsessed with superhero movies and devoured all the books I could get my hands on.

I used to be a lot of things until three years ago when I got hooked on drugs and became a nympho. I don't really know why I did it. I think boredom played a huge factor in my downfall. I was home alone a lot since my boyfriend started traveling a lot for business.

My beauty went away, my success took a shit overnight, and the man that loved me more than he loved himself left me because of my infidelities.

Distraught at what I had become, I turned into a pimp-less whore. I saved enough money to get a small apartment and I got myself clean. I slowly started to rebuild myself and I almost had everything I lost with the exception of Theo. He never did forgive me, but it made me stronger than ever, and I would like to think that's the reason I've survived as long as I have now.

See, I had decided that since Theo couldn't love me anymore and I knew I'd never be able to forgive myself for what I did to him, I left. A year after I got back on my feet, I had saved enough money to do a little globe hopping. Not too many places, but I figured the ones that were closest in proximity would be the places I would go to. Then, I told myself, when I got back from my international adventure I would find a job and keep attending my voluntary rehab sessions. Maybe I could find someone that was just like me and help them. Maybe that would get my mind off of losing the greatest love I knew I would ever have.

It was when touring The Palace of the Grand Masters in Malta that I decided would go home after I visited Camogli and find Theo. I'd tell him everything that I hated about myself for doing what I did to him. I would tell him that he deserved better, he deserved someone who would love him and never stray, and he deserved to be happy. I'd confess that I knew I would never be worth what I was when I was with him. Money, even though I had a lot of it before my mental breakdown, was of no consequence to me anymore. Cars, property, houses; none of it would matter to me anymore because I couldn't share it with him. My final confession would be that I would never feel happiness or worth again. Theo Lennox would always hold a place in my heart, and I knew I would always hold a place in his. I could only hope that he would believe me.

When I left The Palace, I went to the last place on my stop. Camogli had been on the top of my list since I left America because I wanted see the beautiful and colorful homes on the hills and possibly see the *Christ of the Abyss* statue in the harbor of San Fruttuoso.

But I never made it home.

After I had surfaced from my dive the world turned against me. At least that's how it seemed. The family, who had been gracious enough to allow me to rent a room in their home, had my belongings tossed out into the street. No amount of knocking could get them to answer the door and so I grabbed my bags and left.

I remembered being confused, wondering what I had done to be tossed out onto the street, as I made my way through the colorful fishing town trying to find a hostel to stay in.

I remember laying my head down on the limp pillow in the dark little room on the uncomfortable and stiff bed. I remember falling asleep to the sound of whispered voices and I remember holding onto my bag as tightly as I could.

I remembered being afraid, but nothing could prepare me for what true fear was. Nothing could prepare me for waking up in an unfamiliar place and being told by someone I didn't know that he had purchased me and that I was now his property.

I didn't recognize his accent, so I knew I was no longer in Italy. I didn't recognize the city outside the barred windows so I didn't know how

I was going to get home if I couldn't figure out where I was starting from.

I remembered the headache pounding inside my skull, small bursts of bright white light, attacking me every hour, wondering what the hell had been done to me already.

He led me blindfolded to a long wooden table, an iron collar around my neck, and clasped the long chain that had been attached to it to the wall behind me. I was only wearing panties, unsure of what happened to the rest of my clothing. He told me his name was Kerstan and that I would work off the family's debt; the family that let me stay with them in Camogli.

He told me that my name was Lieve and instructed me to forget any past I had, because my future was uncertain. He said that once I paid off the family's debt, he would decide what to do with me.

Like I said; I *used* to be Amity Crane. Now I'm Lieve, red light district whore extraordinaire, to be used at any male or females discretion until I can pay back a debt that was never mine to begin with. A debt that I know nothing about for a family that tricked me into thinking I had found a safe place to live.

As I followed the old, bulgingly, disgusting man into the back room of the whorehouse, I wondered if this would be my last trick before freedom.

I was wrong.

Freedom was never meant to be mine.

ONE

"*GOEDEMORGEN DAMES*," Kerstan said to us as he entered the room. Everyone promptly mumbled their good mornings except for me.

Kerstan Janssen was an absolute sight to look at. Brown straight hair that fell behind his ears, sun-kissed flawless skin, almond shaped light green eyes, a very strong jaw, and a cleft in his chin. True to his heritage he was a tall man and true to his looks, he kept his body well-conditioned and toned.

If this were another time and another place, I would definitely have make a go at Kerstan.

I was sitting on an old spring mattress held up by springs and a bent metal bed frame, in panties only, chained to the wall behind me. That's how we all were when we were in this room. I assumed he had some kind of dominance issues and that's why we were held like this, but I never vocalized it to any of the others.

As I looked around the room at the girls in the room with me who had also been sold to him to settle debt, I wondered how long they had been here. Kerstan had a magnificent collection of beautiful women from all over the world. Some were from Sweden, others from Germany, France, Nepal, Indonesia, and I just so happened to be the stereotypical, token American girl. Almost traditionally "American looking" I had light, long blonde hair, hazel blue eyes, a slender body with a little extra in all the right places, and a million dollar smile. That was me and I was his "best seller."

I pulled my knees up to my chest and wrapped my arms around them. I never minded being almost naked in front of the other girls, but Kerstan wasn't allowed that privilege from me. The only time he had seen me completely naked was when he "assessed" me after bring me back to Amsterdam.

"Why if so many men see you naked and use you at their discretion, am I not allowed to see your breasts?" he once asked me.

"Because you didn't pay for the pleasure of my company," I remember snapping back.

Kerstan chuckled and shook his head, a grin on his face. It was an amusement to him that one of his "girls" was still as headstrong as I was. That was one of the few civilized conversations we ever had. Usually it was him telling me to get ready for my next "date."

But today, right now, he was looking at each of us harshly in turn and when his eyes landed on me, he shook his head slightly and sighed heavily.

"I have to say that I am disappointed in you, dames. I want you all to see this. Then I will punish the one that cannot follow my simple rules," he said pulling something out of his back pocket. I craned my neck to see; my eyebrows furrowed curiously, as he gave the photo to Margit (formerly Bridget, the leggy, blonde Swedish bombshell) and instructed her to pass it around the room.

The girls' eyes would widen or close when

they would look at what I had figured to be a picture before handing it to the next. Since there were only fifteen of us in the group, it didn't take long for me to receive the picture. I was always last in getting anything because I preferred the room closest to the wall away from the door.

Betje (formerly Wendeline, the brown haired braided, freckle faced beauty of Germany) handed me the picture without looking at me. Not that this was the place to make or want friends, but she and I were very close. And because I could see a tear roll down her cheek as she avoided my eyes carefully, I deduced one of two things. Either she was fucked, and I was going to take the punishment for her, or I was fucked, and she would cry through the whole thing.

Survey says... I thought to myself flipping the picture over.

I felt the blood drain from my face as I looked at the photograph, but I kept a steel look on my face. It was a picture of me laughing happily as I tried to get a shot of me and Theo together. All you could see from him was his grin and an arm around my shoulders and it was my favorite picture of us in the entire world.

I glanced up at Kerstan and shrugged.

Showing fear was something that he quite enjoyed, and I wouldn't give it to him. He came to stand at the end of my bed and drummed his fingers along the worn metal frame.

"You know this is not permitted, Lieve," he said softly.

"Then maybe you shouldn't make it so easy," I quipped, tossing the photo back at him.

He chuckled and pulled his hands away from the end of the bed. I watched his eyes grow cold as a sinister smile began to spread across his handsome face.

"How does one punish a girl that just doesn't care?" he mused more to himself than the rest of us.

"Short of setting me on fire, there's nothing you *can* do," I muttered.

"That's not a bad idea actually," he said beginning to pace slowly in front of my bed. Stalk is more likely the correct term for what he was doing honestly. "The two of you are close, correct?" he asked Betje stopping in front of her bed.

She looked up at him nervously. In the middle of her confessing that we were indeed friends, I got to my feet and threw my pillow at her.

"No. We're not. I can't stand the bitch honestly. She's so insipid. I only speak to her to pass the time, but of course even her conversations are fucking boring," I interceded quickly. Kerstan crossed his arms over his shoulders and raised an eyebrow. I quickly hopped onto the mattress and spoke again. "As a matter of fact, I can't stand *any of you bitches*. I hate being in this godforsaken room with you all. I hate that I have to see your miserable faces every fucking day because you're not good enough to fuck your way out of this shit hole. Maybe you should follow me on one of my dates and learn a thing or two."

It was going to be so very difficult to get them to understand that I was doing this to save them. I demeaned each and every one of them as a whole to keep Kerstan from hurting one of them, because he had correctly identified that I didn't give a shit if he did anything to me.

"YOU'RE ALL A BUNCH OF CUNTS!" I yelled throwing both middle fingers into the air.

The girls in the room gasped and looked at me with evil eyes. Apparently I had fooled them into thinking that I was now the biggest bitch they'd ever know; which was the point. Kerstan however was completely unamused.

"Stop embarrassing yourself, Lieve. Off of the bed. *Now,*" he said in a stern voice.

I put my hands on my hips and stared at him defiantly. I was going to pay the price for all of this later but for right now I had to show that I "meant" what I was saying.

"I won't ask you again," he said leaning forward and gripping the edge of the bed frame tightly. Behind him I could see Betje wringing her hands. She was scared for me right now, more than I was scared for myself. I was more concerned for *her*.

"Yes, your majesty," I muttered as I dropped onto the mattress and pulled my knees back up to my chest. He eyed me dangerously for what felt like a lifetime. It was obvious that Kerstan was trying to decide if he was going to punish me just a little or severely. Defiance was not something he tolerated in his home for red light hookers.

I waited nervously now as he began to drum his fingers along the frame. He hadn't taken his stare off of me yet and I was beginning to feel intimidated. I cleared my throat and broke our locked on gazes, conceding this disagreement. *The next one is mine,* I swore to myself.

"Betje, I'd like you to come with me please," he said turning his attention back to her.

"Why?" I blurted out.

Kerstan glanced at me over his shoulder, his green eyes turning cold. But he didn't answer me, then or when he came back with two new girls and no Betje in sight. Not when I broke one of the biggest rules in his little whore camp and pounded on his bedroom door.

Not even when I started banging my fists furiously against his chest. Not even when I started to scream in his face that I wanted to know where Betje was. Not even when he pulled his arm back and punched me as hard as he could in my face, knocking me out cold.

No. Not even then.

I can't say it wasn't unwarranted, but I *can* say that it was a cowardice act. I can also say that because Betje was gone, I was sick of being here, and he had laid his hands on me, that I had set forward an act of retaliation in motion that would echo throughout this house for years to come.

TWO

"THAT LOOKS A LOT BETTER TODAY," Margit said softly, sitting next to me on the bed.

It had been three days since I had taken the sucker punch heard round the world, and the only thing that was wounded was my pride. The swelling had almost gone completely down, and my eye was starting to turn that weird sickly purple and green color. Since I didn't look the part, I couldn't "work," so he let Margit stay with me.

I knew better than to be fooled though. He didn't leave her here with me out of a random act of kindness. He left her here because she was on her period which meant she couldn't work either.

"Does it hurt?" she asked quietly.

I shook my head, "Not anymore."

Margit nodded pushed my hair back so she could get a better look at my eye. "Does not look like he damaged anything," she said peering closely.

"Optometrist, are you?" I asked with a grin.

She laughed and stood up. Moving next to me, she scooted me forward onto the bed so she would have space to sit behind me. A few seconds later, she grabbed two handfuls of hair and began to weave it into a loose braid. I smiled sadly and sighed. There was no such thing as kindness in this place, but Margit knew Betje was my best friend, and I could only assume that she didn't want me to feel alone.

"Don't let him catch you being nice to me," I said quietly.

"What is the worst he can do to me? You and I are his most prized girls. To get rid of either of us would mean that he loses a lot of money. Besides, I'm not afraid of Kerstan," she replied as her fingers continued to weave my hair together.

"Margit? What, um... what's your story?" I

asked nervously. We weren't allowed to talk about our pasts, and even though she was being kind to me at the moment, I didn't trust her still. If she went off and told Kerstan that I had asked her such a forbidden thing, chances were I'd wind up wherever the hell it was that he took Betje.

"My story?" she asked curiously.

"You know, about how you wound up here," I said.

Margit's hands hesitated. I could feel her sudden apprehension. I understood though. It wasn't that she didn't trust me (at least I don't think) it was that she didn't trust this entire situation.

I reached my hands back and undid the braid. I got off of the bed and dropped to my knees, feeling underneath the box spring. When my hand closed around the small rectangular box, I grinned and pulled it out from underneath. I opened the box of cigarettes and pulled one out. I offered one to Margit, but she shook her head. With a shrug, I lit the cigarette and sat on Betje's old bed, one leg up, eyeing Margit.

"Listen, if you're going to tell Kerstan that I asked you that, you might as well tell him about the cigarettes too. Hell, you should probably go tell him now so he can catch me in the act," I said with a smirk.

"I wasn't going to tell him. I just don't want to get talking about things that are forbidden," she replied uncomfortably.

"This entire fucking life is forbidden," I replied with a dry laugh. I placed the cigarette between my lips and lit it, inhaling deeply.

We sat there silently for a moment as I flicked ashes onto the floor. I glanced out the window that sat behind Betje's bed and wondered if she was out there somewhere in the busy city of Amsterdam.

"Did you love her?" Margit asked softly.

"No."

I inhaled deeply again and flicked more ashes onto the floor.

"Then why did you do all that? Purposely degrade the others with words?" she asked.

"Because she's the closest thing I've ever had to a best friend."

I blew out a small succession of smoke rings and watched the last one drift into the window. I chuckled slightly and turned my attention back to Margit.

"I'll tell you my story then. There was this

boy that I loved. Well, he was a man, but for all intents and purposes of poetic love, I'll call him a boy." Inhale. Exhale smoke rings. Ash on the floor. "So anyway, I didn't know what love was until Theo. That was his name, by the way, Theo. Could be because he caught me early on in my life. We were teenagers when we met, high school kids. Early on high school kids. I had suffered a substantial trauma for a consecutive number of years before I met him, and I remembered how big and strong he looked to me and how I felt like he could protect me from it ever happening to me again. I had decided that I wanted him; not as a lover at first, but as a bodyguard of sorts. Of course, I didn't tell him that until after the first time we fucked. See, by that point I was already in love with him. His arms were the safest place to be, and his kisses always tasted like wild honeysuckle. His lips and eyes were always soft, and he never once raised his voice to me in anger. I needed that more than anything and I like to think that he needed me more than anything."

I cleared my throat and looked back out the window, hoping she wouldn't see the single tear that was rolling down my cheek.

"Lieve? You don't have to tell me anymore if you don't want too," she said softly.

"I know," I replied wiping away the tear and taking another drag of my cigarette. "But now that I've started, I want to finish." "Go on," she said in a comforting voice.

I smiled at her briefly, "I fucked up. Plain and simple. But it wasn't because I wanted too; it was because I *had* to. See that trauma I was talking about? It started when I was about seven years old and lasted until I was eleven because that's when puberty hit. She was my piano teacher; yes I said *she*." I took a deep shaky breath and closed my eyes tightly. "She taught me how to use my fingers on the piano and then she used her fingers on *me*. For four fucking years, that bitch would sexually abuse me every time I went to piano lessons and told me that if I ever told my parents, they would hate me forever and then I would have to live with her. And I believed her. So imagine my surprise about twelve years later when Theo and I are at an art gala reception in Woodland Hills and the "artist" just so happens to be *her*. Oh and the best part? She didn't recognize me but apparently had been a friend of Theo's family for years. That kind of set me of off into my downward spiral.

He didn't know of course, because I never told him that it was her. I mean, he knew what had happened to me and he knew that a woman had done those things to me, but never did I tell him who it was. I know it sounds really fucked up that a woman raped me, but it's what *did* happen to me and it's what *does* happen to some girls. And now here I am."

I threw the cigarette onto the floor and used the bottom of my pack to crush it out. I picked up the butt and stuck into my pack, using my feet to kick away the ashes. As long as I remembered to put the cigarettes back into their hiding place, Kerstan wouldn't be able to prove that I was smoking in here even in he could smell it. Fresh tears rolled down my face again and I irritably wiped them away.

"I'm sorry," she said sympathetically.

"For what? Because I'm crying? Don't think I'm shedding a single tear for what happened to me as a kid. I'm not a pity me type of girl. The tears happen whenever I think of Theo.

Whether I want them to or not," I explained getting to my feet.

I walked over to the closet that we kept our "work clothes" in and opened one of the doors. I reached toward the back and jimmied one of the panels until it slid over, and I was able to reach in further to grab what I was looking for. Moments later, I was dressed in an off the shoulder t-shirt and a pair of denim shorts. I pulled on a pair of silver reflecting Ray Ban sunglasses and stuffed the cigarette pack into my back pocket.

"Can you hand me the shoes underneath my bed please?" I

asked Margit. "Just pull up the panel and reach in."

She stared at me for a moment. I knew what she was thinking; that I had special privileges, but the truth of the matter was that I became a genius at hiding all of this shit and an even bigger genius at making myself feel like I was alive on the days that Kerstan wasn't on the property. I rolled my eyes at her suspicious glance and went over to my bed and grabbed my shoes, before setting the panel back and slid them on.

"I'm going out into the gardens for a bit. Do you want to come with me?" I asked her.

She shook her head slightly and went back to her side of the room. I watched her silently wondering if she had plans of ratting me out, but I stopped caring as quickly as I began to wonder.

I walked out of the door without so much as a backwards glance. If Margit wanted to stay in the stale room that smelled like sweat, fear, and the occasional cigarette, that was her problem.

I left her in the room and walked quickly down the empty hall. We were located on the third floor which made the staircase an impossible option, so I learned how to open the window at the end of the hall and lean out the opening toward the giant tree that grazed against the home. I shimmied my way down to the freshly cut green grass and ran toward the gardens. If Kerstan wasn't here, which I prayed he wasn't, then I would have at least an hour outside.

My favorite spot was a stone bench that sat in the shady side that was home to the multicolored pansies. They were small and beautiful and made me the happiest.

I pulled my cigarette pack out of my pocket and placed it between my lips. I leaned my head back and soaked up the peeking rays of the sun, inhaling the scent of the gardens deeply, before lighting the end and putting the lighter back into the pack, before setting it next to me on the bench.

Flicking the first round of ashes onto the

ground, I reached under my sunglasses and gingerly ran the tips of my fingers over my left eye. *At least it doesn't hurt anymore.*

I'll never know what got into me that day that I was out in the gardens, and I'll never know for sure just how long I was asleep on the bench. The only thing I knew for sure was that after Kerstan came back from wherever the hell it was that he went, and found me asleep *outside* of all places, I was in deep shit.

As for Margit ... I never saw her again.

THREE

FOUR DAYS and two new girls later, I was sitting at the large banquet table inside the home. My face was almost completely normal again and Kerstan decided to let us all stay in for the evening so we could get to know each other. I couldn't help but chuckle at this ludicrous dinner. As per custom, we were all topless while he entered the room wearing a baby blue dress shirt, a black vest, and black slacks. And shiny black, obviously expensive, shoes. Even his tie was black and all I could think about besides the fact that we looked like a fucking gangbang waiting to happen, was that if I could get close enough, I could probably choke him to death with that tie.

But I relented and instead sat there with my elbows on the table, and my chin in my hands. The other girls sat around looking completely nervous as he sat down.

"Etiquette, Lieve," he said as he unfolded his napkin.

"Seriously Kerstan? I'm here to fuck whoever you tell me to so you can get your money back. I'm pretty sure they don't give a shit about my table manners," I replied rolling my eyes.

He stared at me for a moment, a small sinister smile crossing

his lips. "They may not, but I do. Elbows off the table."

"Or else what? You'll punch me in the face again? Get rid of another girl that I started to become friends with? Get rid of me, perhaps? No. No, you *wouldn't* get rid of me because you know how much money I bring in for you. Speaking of which, so the new girls here know that you play fair, tell me again, how many more fucks do I owe you before I get out of this hellhole?"

I asked defiantly.

Kerstan set his napkin down on his lap neatly

before folding his hands in front of him looking at me in amusement. I could feel the tension and smell the fear on the other girls. I personally knew that he wouldn't do much more to me because that would keep me out of his book and I'm sure that my regular "clients" had been requesting my company.

"Lieve, why do you test me?" he asked.

"Because I don't see you out there fucking off a debt. Oh did you guys know that I'm working off someone else's mess? Yeah I was dumb enough to stay with a family that I thought was doing me a kindness. I came back one day and boom! My shit was out in the street, and I wound up staying in a hostel, that I'm still convinced is owned by that one," I said jerking my thumb in his direction.

"Lieve, you're excused," Kerstan said in a stern voice.

"Maybe I don't want to leave," I replied, crossing my arms over my chest, and leaning back against the chair. "Maybe I think

I deserve an answer first."

You know that expression about playing with fire? Well the look in Kerstan's eyes told me that I was teetering at the edge of a volcano with molten lava waiting to swallow me whole. But he didn't lose his temper and he didn't get up from his seat. Instead he leaned forward and clasped his hands on the table before answering me.

"Just one big one that you'll never forget."
What the hell does that mean?

"Of course, you'll continue to work until that one is ready for you. I can't have you getting rusty, though I will allow one month's rest before you are to satisfy the arrangement so that you tighten up," he finished with a smirk.

I stared at him. *One more with a bunch of little ones in between. Why am I not surprised?* But if that was the case, then I shouldn't have to "work" anymore until that one was ready for me.

"Can I object to that? I mean, if there's only one more then why don't you give me that rest starting today and then I can get it over with," I said reasonably.

Kerstan laughed as he reached for his glass of blood red wine. He took a hearty drink before setting it down and looking at me with his evil eyes.

"You misunderstand, Lieve. You will not be going out to work until it's time. You're now going to be *mine* to use until the final encounter is set," he replied.

"Y...yours?" I stammered in shock.

A somewhat sinister smile crossed his lips as he took another drink from his wine glass. He held my gaze as he set his glass down and nodded. Then he turned his attention to the rest of the girls in the room, new and seasoned.

"Does this answer your questions, dames? Do not think that what Lieve must do is something you will all endure. What you will do is work off the debts owed to me and then I will let you leave. But let's not speak of business anymore; instead let us enjoy the feast that I have planned for you all. The food will arrive shortly. Speak amongst yourselves until then," he said in a faux pleasant tone.

As the girls quietly started speaking amongst themselves, I found the courage inside of me to do something that we were never allowed to do without permission. I got to my feet, and I walked down the length of the table with my chair, and sat it down next to Kerstan. I folded my hands in my lap and thought carefully about the words that were going to come out of my mouth. And about the gleaming blade of the sharp knife that sat by the plate at his setting.

"Why are you doing this to me?" I asked quietly. "It seems

like this is more of a personal vendetta than a debt."

"Would you like some wine?" he asked, holding out an empty glass. I watched as one of the older grandmotherly women (who I assumed to have been indebted for quite some time now) came forward and filled the glass with red wine.

He handed me the glass and I set it down, my eyes lingering on the knife for a moment. *If I kill him, I'll be stuck here forever. I know it,* I thought tearing my eyes away and looking at him.

"I never did much care for blonde hair," he said absently as he took a hand full of my hair gently in his hand. "Would you mind terribly changing it for me?"

"Kerstan," I said pulling my hair out of his hand, "Just let me do the final fuck. Please. I want to go home."

"Reduced to begging, are you? I thought you were stronger than that, Lieve. I thought you had more will than becoming a beggar," he replied with a smirk. "But to answer your request, my answer is *neen*. This is not something you can bargain your way out of. You will wait until the appropriate moment and in the meantime, you will be my *seksspeeltje*. Understand?"

I blinked back bitter tears. I had no idea what the fuck that meant, but I sure as hell understood the word "neen." He had yelled it enough times in frustration with some of the girls that used to be here.

"I'm going to my room. I'm getting dressed and I'm going back out to the gardens. I *will* be smoking and actually, I'll be needing a pack soon. If you want me to be your *seksspeeltje* then I expect some perks. I can tell that there will be no way out of this than to go with the flow. So allow me some small comforts,"

I said getting to my feet.

Kerstan cleared his throat and drank the rest of his wine as a small group of elderly women came out with trays of food. I eyed the small feast hungrily as they placed tray after tray down, uncovering it and revealing all of the delicious meats, fruits, and various gravies.

I had to put a hand firmly on my stomach to silence the low grumble that escaped. Here I was trying to be a big bitch and my insides were giving me away.

"I want my name back. I want to be called Amity in this house since I no longer have to go out and fuck for you. Also, I want Betje back. Those are my terms," I said putting my hands on my hips.

Kerstan finished putting a couple of thick slices of roast pork on his plate, before setting down his fork and knife. He wiped his mouth with his napkin and got to his feet.

Whatever happens, don't be scared, I told myself, trying to give him a level stare.

"Come with me," he said, taking me by the elbow and half dragging me out of the massive dining room.

We had only stepped into the hallway outside the dining room but for some reason I still didn't trust the situation. If he hit me again, I was going to rip his hands off.

As Kerstan closed the door firmly behind us I looked around the room seeing if there would be anything I could use to protect myself.

"Lieve —"

"*Amity,*" I corrected firmly.

He chuckled and dug his hands into his pockets. "*Amity;* there are some things you must understand. Once I trade a girl I cannot get her back. Betje is out of the question. As for your name, if you wish it, I will address you as Amity in private, but in front of the others, you *are* Lieve. I don't want them to start to riot over simplicities. Because you are mine for the time being, they will already resent you for not having to out and work. Do we have an agreement?"

Of all the things I wanted back more than my own identity was Betje. It would be the only way I knew she would be safe and sound. *When I get out of this shit hole, I'll find her.*

I stuck my hand out to confirm our agreement. Kerstan gave me a half smile as he took my hand in his and shook it firmly. As I attempted to pull my hand away, he pulled me against him with a sudden jerk.

"When I'm fucking you, what do I call you then?" he whispered into my ear.

I closed my eyes as my body reacted to the softness of his voice and the strength that he used to keep me against him with one hand. *Oh God, how is that I hate him but ... parts of me wants this? Stop reacting!* I mentally screamed at the "come fuck me" senses that were tingling deep inside of me.

Kerstan finally let me go and gave me an amused look. I knew he could see my nipples standing at attention because I couldn't exactly hide them. I also couldn't hide the beginnings of the pool in my panties, so I turned and ran.

Back to my room.

Away from Kerstan.

I locked the door behind me tightly and laid down on my bed. I slid my hand into my panties and immediately began to rub with my clit. The small amount of dominance he had just shown had thrown me into pure fucking mode and I had to cum, STAT. I slid my fingers in and out of myself, rubbing my clit faster as I felt it starting to tense up. When I finally came, his gorgeous face burned into my memory and wondering what someone who owns a place like this was sexually capable of, I felt myself die a little on the inside.

FOUR

I DIDN'T LEAVE the room until the next day. Most of the girls had been sent out on "dates" and I was too embarrassed about having finger fucked myself to thoughts of our "pimp" to even look at any of them.

"Are you okay, Lieve?" a small voice asked once the room was almost empty.

I had been lying on my side staring at the wall. I can't say that I was ashamed of myself really, I mean like I said before, different circumstances presented, I would've fucked him already, but

... This shit is getting too weird for me.

"Lieve?" the voice asked again.

With a heavy sigh I turned on my side and sat up. Crossing my legs underneath myself I looked at the young woman sitting at the end of my bed. She was looking at me with concerned doe eyes; light brown to be exact. Her blonde hair was pulled back into a tight ponytail and her face was flawless.

"What's your name?" I asked her.

"The name I was born with was Helenka," she said quietly.

"My new name is Minikin."

"And where are you from, *Minikin*?" I asked.

"The Czech Republic," she replied proudly.

"Well *Minikin*, don't expect to be my friend. Or talk to me again after this conversation is over for that matter. People that I get close to, even just a little close to tend to disappear," I said tiredly.

"Why do you keep saying my name like that?" she asked in confusion.

"Because I don't want you to follow my lead and ask to do by your birth name. Kerstan is not one for games or jokes or anything that seems pleasant or joyful really, and he'll take that as a sign of rebellion. God knows what'll happen to you then."

Before this is over, I'm going to make him tell me what Betje did to him that was so offensive that he sold her. And I want to know to who, I thought darkly to myself.

She looked at me like I was lying, or maybe like I was full of myself. I wasn't sure which yet, but it was her ass that would be handed off to someone else; not mine. With a shrug, I reached under the bed and felt around until my hands clasped around the cigarette box holding my last smoke. I shook out the lighter and tossed the empty box onto the bed before lighting my cigarette and inhaling deeply.

This was a clusterfuck and I hated it. In no way shape or form, did I want to be having any desires for Kerstan that weren't murderous, but the way he ... My body shivered at the memory, and I turned my attention back to Minikin.

"How old are you?" I asked her.

"Nineteen."

Figures. That seems to be the age most of these girls are, I thought with a scoff.

"I hope you've had sex already honey, because you do *not* want your cherry popped by one of those vicious bastards," I said, flicking the ashes of my cigarette onto the floor.

She turned her face away and sniffled. *Oh fuck. She is a virgin. Think of something quick, Amity.*

I sighed and brought my knee up, resting my arm on top of it. There had to be a way to save this girl from the horrors of being one of Kerstan's whores. I glanced around the room trying to brainstorm when her sudden sob distracted me.

"Whatever you do, never let him see you cry," I warned holding up a finger. "Not that you should have to worry about that. I'm going to get you out of here, but you're going to have to pull it together for me. Can you do that?"

"Why would you help me?" she asked suddenly.

That's a good question. Because I can't help myself? Because I couldn't help Betje? Because one of us should make it out of here unscathed?

"Let's just say it'll be the only good deed that someone will remember me for," I replied quietly looking out the window. I took another drag of my cigarette, only to find that in my master-minding the break out of Minikin, I had let it burn down to the filter. I looked down on my bed and sighed, sliding the ashes onto the floor. "That was my last one too," I said with a rueful smile.

"Lieve, *uw aanwezigheid wordt gevraagd*," one of the grandmothers as I was now calling them said, poking her head into the room.

I glanced at her and nodded. I didn't understand all of what she said, but I did manage to catch the gist of it. I was being summoned and there was only one person in this house who would want to see me.

"I want you to stay here until I get back, Minikin. If anyone opens that door, you go out that window and down that tree. Go hide in the gardens; I'll be able to find you there. Okay?" I asked getting to my feet.

She nodded and I gave her a small smile, before turning on my heel and walking out of the room. I closed the door behind me firmly and followed the grandmother toward the far west side of the home. We walked around a corner that was so well hidden, that you'd never know it was there unless you were privileged to the information.

But it was more obvious than being "summoned" that we were on our way to Kerstan's room. Which meant he wanted to start his sexual adventures with me tonight. Which meant that

Minikin was going to be on her own and if she went into the gardens, I probably wouldn't be able to get to her until tomorrow. *Fuck.*

The grandmother led me to a pair of beautiful wooden double doors at the end of the dimly lit hallway and gestured for me to enter. I put one hand on the elaborate gold tone doorknob and bit my lower lip nervously.

My hesitation was not a deterrent to the grandmother who took the decision from me when she put her hand on mine and opened the door, giving me a gentle shove inside.

Kerstan was sitting in a grand leather chair by the window, one leg crossed atop the other, while he held a glass of wine in one hand, still in his exquisite clothing from the Feast of the New Flesh. Of course he didn't call it that, but I did. I had been through enough new girls here that I just started making names up for certain things. I could see from his gaze that something outside had caught his attention, but I didn't care enough to allow myself to become curious.

He took a sip of wine before he spoke, "What took so long?"

My inner fear gave way to annoyance almost immediately.

"Apologies, your Highness, I didn't realize we were under a time crunch here," I replied sarcastically.

A laugh escaped from somewhere inside of him; the first I ever heard from Kerstan. I rolled my eyes nonetheless, and pulled my panties off. I tossed them to the side and went to his lush king sized bed and climbed on. I made myself comfortable somewhere in the middle of it and cleared my throat.

"Lieve, may I ask you something?"

"You promised to call me Amity when we were alone," I reminded him in a cold tone.

"Amity. So, may I?" He took another sip of wine and never tore his eyes off of whatever he was looking at outside.

"Sure."

"Was Betje your lover?"

"What? No! Why would you think that?" I asked in shock.

"Because you tried to bargain for her return. I simply assumed you to be lovers," he replied setting his now empty glass down on the floor next to him.

"She was my *friend,*" I replied, emphasizing the word.

He nodded. I pushed my hair behind my ears and sighed. I wondered how long it would take for him to do something I had no desire to do.

"And Margit?"

"We were getting there. To being friends I mean," I replied.

"What of Minikin? She seemed a bit distraught when I excused you yesterday," he said conversationally.

"Because she's scared, Kerstan. She doesn't want to be here anymore than the rest of us do. We're not friends though. I already told her not to even attempt to be my friend because I have zero interest."

Kerstan chuckled and finally got to his feet. I closed my eyes tightly for a moment and told myself not to fight him; to let him do whatever he wanted to me. But when the bed didn't creak and when I didn't hear the sound of his pants unzipping, I cracked one eye open and glanced over at him. He had his hands pressed firmly on the windowsill and he was looking at something almost directly below him.

"Come here," he said without looking at me.

I took a deep breath and shimmied toward the end of the bed. I quickly walked over to Kerstan's side, and he finally turned to glance at me. His smile gave me chills, because it was the sinister smile he would almost always get when he was going to say or do something completely fucked up.

He turned slightly and sat on the windowsill keeping his eyes glued to my face. I raised an eyebrow at his intent stare and wondered how high up we really were and if a jump would kill or just maim me.

"So, Minikin is of no consequence to you, then?" he asked.

"None," I lied, licking my lips nervously.

With a nod, he reached into his pocket and pulled out a cell phone. I watched as he pressed a button, held the phone to his ear, and after a short moment, said something in Dutch. No sooner did he hang up his phone than I heard a scream from outside. Curiously, I got as close as I could to Kerstan so that I could look outside. And when I looked down, my heart broke, and tears sprang to my eyes.

It was Minikin. Sweet virginal Minikin, surrounded by a small group of men. Instinctively, I tried to push past Kerstan because I reasoned there had to be some way to get down into the gardens that I now knew sat below his window, and save her from what was about to happen. But he gripped my wrists tightly in his arms, and sat me down on the small sliver of space next to him.

"Watch."

That was his simple command. His only wish for this entire evening tonight was that I would watch. One of them looked up at the window at Kerstan, almost as if waiting for approval. I wasn't sure if he gave a nod, because my back was pressed against his body, but the man grabbed Minikin by her hair and lifted her head.

When she saw me she burst into tears. This young girl who trusted me, or at least I thought she did, was looking up at her owner and her pseudo friend sitting on the windowsill "together" watching.

"Kerstan, please don't do this to her. *Please,* she's a virgin. This isn't right. This shouldn't happen to her," I whispered frantically to him.

He chuckled behind me, and let one hand slide from my left wrist, around my waist. "I don't like being lied to *Amity.* Your foolishness is what costs her purity. I will not tell them to be gentle and I will not stop them. I want them to bruise her on the inside and I want her to know that you had a hand in it. And do you know why? Because you think yourself my equal and it drives me mad. If you wish to be my equal, then you will learn how.

At the expense of those close to you," he whispered into my ear.

I watched as the man let go of her hair and pushed her roughly to the ground. I watched as he ripped her panties from her body, and I watched as he took his erection out of his pants and position himself behind her.

"Let me take her place," I pleaded.

"No. You're still a whore, but you're now *my* whore until it is time to give you up. Now. *Watch.*" And I did.

As each man climbed on top of her after her initial, brutal pounding that she took. After she had her virginity stolen from her in the worse way possible, I sat and I watched as each of the men took turns viciously raping Minikin; sometimes two at a time, as she cried helplessly until her tears and sobs faded away to nothing. Until she just lay in the gardens that I once loved so much and took violation after violation, a stoic, faraway look on her face.

FIVE

I WAS LYING in Kerstan's bed, the sounds of Minikin's screams and sobs echoing loudly in my mind. As loud as a sonic boom exploding over and over in my mind. I knew the sun would be up soon and I would hopefully be allowed to go back to our rooms. I decided that I would convince Minikin to run away with me; I wanted to set her free more now than ever and I would come back so that he wouldn't send anyone to chase her.

The sun had not yet come up when Kerstan stirred behind me. His fingers came to life and slowly rubbed my belly before he removed his hand to my hip.

"*Goedemorgen,*" he said softly.

"Not quite," I replied curtly. I grit my teeth to keep myself from attempting to break his hand. His touch to me was viler than that of any of the "customers" I had been sent to entertain.

He chuckled tiredly and took his hand from my hip, using it to brush my hair away from my face and neck. Kerstan shifted slightly and gently grazed his lips against my neck, causing my body to react. My mind, however, was wondering how long I would be able to take this before I tried to impale him with the pen that was sitting on the nightstand next to us.

He shifted again, pressing himself against me, and I immediately became outraged. I could feel his erection firmly behind his pants and I wanted to drive an elbow down into it.

But even though he knew how violently angry I was at him for what happened to Minikin, he gently pressed his lips against my neck, causing me to squirm slightly. *Fuck. No, no, no. Do NOT give this bastard the satisfaction,* I screamed at myself as he used his hand to gently cup my breast. His forefinger and thumb closed around my nipple, and he squeezed it gently, before giving it a pull. My breath came out in a shuddery gasp when he turned me over onto my back.

"Is it a good morning yet?" he asked with a half tired smile before leaning forward and taking my nipple into his mouth.

Don't react. Don't react. DO NOT REACT.

"Not quite," I said again, closing my eyes tightly and balling my fists at my side.

I felt his smile on me before he gently nibbled on my nipple. The bed bounced slightly as he moved his body down. Knowing what he was going to do, I locked my knees together like a bear trap. No way in hell was he going to do *anything* to me that I didn't want.

"It'll be worth it, Amity. I promise," he said gently as he pulled my legs apart. Kerstan was a lot stronger than I thought he was. My legs gave way without so much as a slight struggle.

And then I heard it. The sound I was waiting for last night; the zipper coming undone. I heard his belt clink slightly as he un-looped it and the sound of the fabric of him sliding his pants and underwear off.

I grunted when he pushed himself inside of me. Kerstan was a big boy, bigger than I ever had anyway, but not big enough to tear anything. Not that he could; I'd had so many cocks and toys in there in the past year, that I was surprised I could still feel anything.

"I can't do this if you won't look at me," he said with a laugh. The friendly laugh; not the evil laugh. For a moment, I forgot that he was a monster and let my eyes open.

His haunting green eyes went from dancing with laughter to absolute lust as our eyes locked and I found myself lost in them. He pushed inside of me again, a little gentler than the first, and I let my hands find their way to his sides. I found myself grabbing at his shirt, trying to pull it off of him, while he began to rhythmically thrust in and out of me. I wrapped my legs around him and pulled harder at his shirt, getting it halfway up over him, when he gripped me and turned us over. Kerstan pulled his shirt back down before putting his hands on my hips and looking at me with commanding eyes. I closed mine and leaned my head back as I started to move on top of him.

His breathing became unsteady as he started to thrust upward. I opened my eyes and gave him a grin, leaning forward to balance myself on his shoulders, and began to bounce up and down on his cock causing him to close *his* eyes, and moan loudly.

I moved harder and faster than I ever had. I don't know what had come over me, other than my desperate need to please him. Kerstan reached up and grabbed my breasts and squeezed them tightly, his hands like vice grips as I continued to bounce on his cock.

A euphoric gasp escaped my lips as I felt the orgasm building deep inside of me. How was it possible that this man that I hated so much could make me cum so quickly? One more bounce, two, three, the fourth being met with him ramming his cock up inside of me and I gripped his arms tightly as my insides tightened up, before releasing my juices all over his cock.

My breath came in pants as I held onto him until the orgasm subsided and I was able to some-what regain control of my body. I closed my eyes for a moment and laughed; something I always did after I came and let go of his arms.

"*Mooi*," he said quietly.

I opened my eyes and looked at him. *Oh. You're still here.* I climbed off of him and sat next to him on the bed, my legs stretched out in front of him. It couldn't have lasted more than ten minutes, but

I think I was able to cum because I had somehow managed to convince myself subconsciously that Kerstan wasn't Kerstan.

"What does that mean?" I asked, examining my fingernails.

"It means beautiful," he explained, pulling himself up to sit next to me.

How the hell can he still be hard? I wondered sneaking a peek at his cock.

"Did you cum?" I asked him. "No." *That's how.*

"Sorry. Guess I'm not as good as I thought I was," I replied with a shrug.

"Don't apologize. You were magnificent, but if I am not in control of the situation when I'm fucking, then I can't cum," he said simply.

Figures, I thought with an internal eye roll.

There was a soft tap at the door and Kerstan sighed. He got to his feet and pulled his pants and underwear on before reaching down for my panties and tossing them at me. *Just like a trick; he's done with me and now it's time to go.* I got to my feet and pulled them on, before I sat down on the edge of the bed waiting to be dismissed.

He opened the door slightly and leaned a hand against the adjacent door as he poked his head out. I couldn't hear what was being said, but the soft tone and the Dutch told me that it was clearly one of the grandmothers. I watched curiously as his body stiffened and he leaned his head back, a sigh escaping his body. He nodded before closing the door securely behind him and kept his back to me, hand still against the door.

"Amity, come here please," he said quietly.

A bad feeling began to wash over me like a waterfall, as I got to my feet and made my way to him. As I neared him, I could almost swore that I heard him swear under his breath, but he used one hand to quickly wipe his face clean of any evidence of emotion before he turned to face me.

"I must travel to Utrecht this afternoon. I have a pressing matter to attend to. I will return this evening," he said.

"Why are you telling *me* this?" I asked in confusion.

"Because I want you to know why I will be gone. And to ensure that nothing foolish happens in my absence," he said pointedly.

I nodded in understanding. In other words, he didn't want me to think this would be a good time to break any of the girls out.

Minikin.

"Am I excused, Kerstan? I'd like to get back to my room and um ...," my voice trailed off, not finding the right words to lie with.

"Yes. But she isn't there. She's in the Care Room where she is not granted visitors. Do you understand me?" he asked, grabbing me by an arm.

I nodded and he let me go. Kerstan stepped aside, allowing me to leave his room, and I found a grandmother waiting to escort me back to the room all of his glorious hookers shared.

I thanked her after she left me there and had I known how truly tragic the evening was going to turn; I would've followed my gut instinct and went to the Care Room. I would've told Minikin that I wanted nothing more to help her. I would've told her that she was still of much worth. I would've told her that somehow it was going to be okay.

But I never did go, and it was something that I would regret and hate myself for later on.

SIX

"GOD, I wish I spoke the fucking language around here!" I shouted angrily as I sat down on my bed feeling defeated.

I had just come back from desperately trying to coerce one of the grandmothers into letting me into the Care Room, but the language barrier and probable heads up from Kerstan, made it beyond impossible.

I reached under my bed for my cigarettes and let out a shout of frustration when I pulled out an empty pack. If ever there was a time that I needed some nicotine it was at that exact moment. I crushed the pack in my hand before I threw it across the room. The other girls stole glances at me before starting to gossip amongst themselves. Christ only knows what they've heard, but what they've seen so far holds true; any of them who get close to me get punished and I didn't know why.

There has to be some way to get down to her. There has to be some way to let her know that I was forced to sit there and watch what happened to her.

"Dames?" an elderly voice called out, snapping me out of my thoughts.

I turned my attention to the door and the eldest of all the grandmothers was standing in the center of the room, while the others dispersed dresses to us.

"When Kerstan returns tonight, he will have with him his wife," she said in slow, broken English. "You are to not speak a word of what this home is for. She believes it to be a boarding school and you will present yourselves as such. Am I understood?"

The other girls nodded, while I stared at her incredulously. *He's married? And this is a boarding school? Is his wife that fucking stupid?*

"There will be many consequences for any of

you who break these rules tonight," she warned before leaving the room behind the other grand-mothers.

When she left, I put my dress on, an idea formulating in my mind. No way in hell was I going to let this go on for any longer than it had to. I would bargain with Kerstan; let me take Minikin away from this place and his little, shitty secret would be safe with me. If he didn't I would expose him to his wife and watch the fire burn.

Dusk fell quickly and the girls and I were led to the dining room again. We were all seated like proper little things when Kerstan entered to room with an extremely elegant woman on his arm. To say she was beautiful would be an understate-ment; to say she was a goddess would be almost perfect.

"Dames, this is my Xandra Janssen, my wife," Kerstan said to us.

I was too busy staring at her to care what her name was. She was almost as tall as Margit was and had dark red curls that fell to her back. Her lips were painted dark red to match her hair and her big brown eyes were kind and unassuming. I would compare her skin to ivory; smooth, flawless, and impossibly pale. She was dressed as extraordinarily as Kerstan was and they looked more like they were going to a ball than to have dinner with us.

All of the other girls brightly greeted her, but I sat back in my chair and folded my arms over my chest. Xandra didn't notice my lack of manners, but Kerstan did, and his gaze turned to stone when it settled on me.

"I'm Lieve," I said getting to my feet and extending a hand.

"Hello Lieve!" she replied in a bright voice, shaking my

hand. "It is a pleasure to meet you!"

"Same," I grinned. "Please, have a seat. I would *love* to get to know you."

She smiled widely at Kerstan as she took the seat beside him, which just so happened to be the one that was almost directly across from me. I had planned it perfectly because I wanted him to hear my words. Much like what Minikin believed, I wanted Xandra to believe that I had a hand in this because then it would make sense as to why I had slept with her husband the night before.

The grandmothers entered the room and poured glasses of wine for everyone. Xandra held Kerstan's left hand and chatted animatedly in

Dutch. Since she gestured around the table a few times, I assumed she was impressed with everything he had done.

"You know, I've never seen you here before," I said interrupting their conversation.

"Oh! I visit the school once a year but stay in Utrecht while

Kerstan travels between both places," she said pleasantly.

I nodded and raised the glass of wine to my lips to hide my smile. Out of the corner of my eye, I could see the sweat starting to appear on Kerstan's brow. It was obvious to him what I was going to do, and I knew that if I didn't do this right, I'd probably wind up dead.

"Do you like this school?" she asked, leaning back in her chair, and sipping her wine.

"This is definitely not like any other 'school' I've attended. Doesn't take much to get on the Dean's List, does it Kerstan?" I asked, glancing at him.

"Lieve, may I have private words with you?" he asked suddenly.

I nodded and pushed my chair back, while he kissed his wife's hand before getting to his feet and leading me out of the dining room.

"Banished to the hallway again?" I asked, putting my hands on my hips after he closed the door behind us.

In the blink of an eye, a vicious slap turned my face. Instinct told me to slap him back, which I did.

"You little bitch," he growled, grabbing me by the hair and slamming me against the wall. The smack of the back of my head against the hard wooden wall blinded me momentarily. But the sudden engulfment of his lips smashing against mine excited me.

I don't know why. I'll never know why, but Kerstan's touch did something to me that I couldn't find a way to control. I gripped his sides and pulled him harder against me, eagerly and viciously returning his rough kiss. But he pulled away from me as quickly as he kissed me, leaving me standing there, a puddle in my panties, and pinning my arms over my head.

"What do you want from me?" he asked in a husky voice, dripping with desire.

"Minikin; I want to take her away from here before she becomes any more damaged than she already is," I replied in a shaky tone.

He put his hand around my chin and kissed

me again. Passionately, hungrily; everything that I wanted and missed from Theo was now in the form of a man I detested and secretly wished dead. He pressed his desire against me, and I wanted him more in that moment than my mind ever wanted anything. Mentally, I was fucked right now.

"No," he whispered when he pulled away.

The lust I was feeling for Kerstan died in that one word. I twisted my arms away from his grip and gave him a shove, causing him to almost fall over as I walked back into the dining room.

"This isn't a school," I announced in a loud voice stopping next to Xandra. The girls gasped, the grandmothers looked terrified, and her? Well she just looked confused.

"Lieve!" Kerstan warned harshly as he entered behind me.

I looked at him over my shoulder, "Last chance. I want

Minikin."

"No," he said again, his voice shaking in anger.

"Suit yourself," I replied with a shrug. "Xandra, I hate to be the one to tell you this, but like I said this isn't a school."

"Amity," Kerstan said in a much softer tone. "Don't do this."

"*This,* my dear Mrs. Janssen, is a whore house, run by *your* husband, and *we* are his whores. He orchestrated the gang rape of a *virgin* who I had promised to keep safe. Oh, and I'm sorry to tell you this, but we fucked this morning. He never mentioned he had a wife and I'm his personal slut until I get to the Final

Fuck as I've come to call it and get the hell out of here."

I sat down in Kerstan's chair after my grand-standing was over and watched Xandra's face turn from interested to horrified. She got up from her chair and looked frantically around the room. "Is this true?" she asked the other girls, who all looked away.

"That's a 'yes.' They're all just too scared of him to say shit," I said nodding at Kerstan who was now standing in between me and Xandra.

Kerstan reached out for Xandra, but she shrank away from me. With a sigh, he reached for one of the elaborate metal trays that sat on the table, dumped the food off of it, and cracked it against her face. She fell to floor in a crying, bloody heap and he motioned for the grand-mothers to take her. He let the tray fall to the floor before taking the seat where she had been.

"Why do you defy me so?" he asked quietly.

Okay if he did that to his wife, I need to start reeling in the sarcasm and shit, I thought watching two grandmothers help her to her feet and walk her out of the room.

"Lieve, you were warned against that. You were asked not to do this one simple thing and yet you did it anyway. What pleasure do you achieve in defying me?" he asked with a shout, and slam-ming his fist against the table.

He's like a sexy Dr. Jekyll and Mr. Hyde who's gone on the fucking crazy train!

Then something hit me like a ton of bricks; metaphorically speaking. She wasn't his wife. She couldn't be. She said she visited the school once a year and this was the first time I had ever seen her. So then who the hell was she?

"New recruit?" I asked nervously.

The smile appeared on his face; the one that made me cringe.

The smile gave way to a grin, and he nodded.

Fuck. It was a test and I failed. But at what price?

"M ... Minikin?" I asked hesitantly.

"Of no concern to you or me ever again. She will of course be punished for your little display. Six men may have felt like a lot to you before, so this time I will see to it that it is doubled. This was your choice to defy me and now you see that not everything is always as it seems. You will retire to my room tonight and we will look out over the gardens as we did the night before," he said before he stood and left the room.

SEVEN

I WAS KNEELING in front of the toilet, wiping away the spit from my mouth with a rolled up piece of toilet paper. I had left the "dinner" of my own will and spent that time until now throwing up. If we were going to watch the gardens that meant that Minikin was going to get raped again and there would be nothing I could do to stop it. I couldn't deal with it again, not a second time.

"Lieve, come," one of the grandmothers said, appearing in the doorway of the bathroom. I waved her away without so much as gracing her with a glance. No way in hell was I going to see this shit go down; he would have to watch it by himself.

"You refuse?" she asked curiously.

"Fuck off," I barked, turning to glare at her over my shoulder.

She immediately left the doorway. I knew this wasn't going to sit well with *him*, but I honestly just didn't care. A few moments later, I hung my head over the bowl again and another bought of fluids came out of me. Tears stained my face and I felt myself becoming exhausted. I closed my eyes and leaned back against the wall, after I cleaned my mouth again and tossed the paper into the toilet.

A hand gently touched my shoulders and my eyes snapped open. It was Janneke (real name and authentic Dutch woman) looking at me with her blue eyes full of concern. She was one of the only ones I could remember being here before me, but we had never spoken two words to each other.

"Get away from me," I said weakly. "You'll disappear. Or worse, you'll end up like Minikin. Please. I'll be okay, just get away from me."

She nodded and her hand left my shoulder. I closed my eyes again and sat there, feeling the fatigue take over me and trying to lull me to sleep when Kerstan's voice robbed me of my almost sleep about a half an hour later.

"Amity?" he asked, pulling the door to the bathroom closed behind him.

"Fuck off."

He chuckled as he sat down next to me on the dirty bathroom floor. I opened my eyes and rolled my head slowly in his direction. He was looking at me in mostly amusement and partial concern.

"Careful. You don't want to dirty one of your fancy outfits sitting on this disgusting floor with a mere whore," I said tiredly.

"Why do you think so little of me?" he asked curiously.

"I don't have the time or the strength right now to get into that list," I snapped.

Kerstan laughed (the friendly laugh) and scooted closer to me. I tried to move away from him but found myself stuck between him and the damn toilet bowl with no extra room to maneuver away.

"That dress becomes you," he said politely.

I glared at him, "Shouldn't you be off setting up Minikin's next gang rape?"

Kerstan let out a deep and wounded sigh. He

ran a hand back through his hair before reaching for my left hand and holding onto it firmly.

"I know that I act dominant sometimes and I know that I am always not pleasant to you or anyone who you become close with. But these are not my actions of free will. This is what I am instructed to do to you, Amity. Until it is time for you to leave me," he explained quietly.

Wait a minute.

"You mean someone is telling you to do all of this shit to me?" I asked. "Who is it?"

"That's not your concern. Not yet, anyway," Kerstan replied shaking his head. "I get paid a great deal of money for the other girls and their services, but for you ... See, you are a special case. I am to break you down more and more each day and report back to your new owner. Each day I get paid a greater interest sum for what I report back. I can't send a defiant girl to a man who is paying such a price, so to break you, I will destroy everything around you and make you feel more pain than you've ever physically or emotionally have felt."

"Why do I have to fuck you in the meantime?" I asked, an enormous headache suddenly taking over.

"That's just for fun. I've had you here for a long time and was not, until recently, given the okay to start your break down and reconstruction. Until then I was not allowed to touch you, but now I am," he explained with a smile.

I broke down sobbing. It wasn't because I was sad and it wasn't because I was set up, it was because I allowed my actions to hurt others around me again. I was such a failure at being a good person and I only cared about myself. And that's what drove Theo away. That's what took Betje and Margit away from the home and what cost Minikin her virginity in such a brutal fashion.

"Shh, don't cry," he said putting his arm around my shoulders. "I appear a bastard around the others because I have to be stern with them. They fear me because they know what I am now capable of with you. But I allow you certain privileges, such as your name and wandering freely in the gardens, because I see

how greatly you care for the others, when I cannot."

"I don't want to do this anymore," I said through my sobs. "I just want this to be done and over with. Please, Kerstan, I'm begging you to let me take Minikin away from here. I'll come back, I promise you, I'll come back, but she doesn't deserve to suffer because of my arrogance."

"I can't allow that," he replied quietly.

An instant bout of nausea rolled over me, causing me to lunge for the bowl again. This was a no win situation. I was stuck fucking a man I hated, but thoroughly seemed to enjoy the act. I promised a girl that I would do my best to protect her and get her out of here, but only sit and watch while men force themselves on her.

"Who is it?" I gasped, reaching for some more toilet paper to clean my mouth. "Who is doing this to me?"

Instead of answering me, he stood up and got me to my feet. He reached for another few pieces of paper and cleaned my mouth completely before tossing his and mine in the toilet and flushing it. Kerstan turned the faucet on and checked the temperature of the water before he slightly bent me over and began to wash my face for me. When he was done, he pulled off his fancy vest and wiped my face dry.

I looked at him and wondered how he could be so gentle and assumingly caring in one moment but smash a tray in someone's face a few moments before? What was wrong with him?

"What can I do to convince you to let me take her away?" I asked stubbornly.

Kerstan sighed heavily and shook his head. I wanted to save what was left of her. I wanted something that I had broken to have a chance to be fixed and something to be able to love being alive again.

"I can't let her out of this life per se, but if it makes you rest easier, I can arrange to have her go where Betje went; to a kinder house," he said, looking into my eyes.

My lower lip trembled, but I felt a smile cross my face. Betje would take care of her once Minikin said my name. *If* she would even mention me.

"Can I write a letter to Betje? To let her know I've been thinking about her? Please?" I asked.

Kerstan nodded, "So then you agree to this? Minikin is to go where Betje went?"

Do I have a choice?

"Yes. I agree. But I want her to go tonight. And I want to be able to say good-bye."

Kerstan smiled, "You ask for too many things, Amity. She cannot leave until it is arranged. That will take at least a day or two. I will allow you to say good-bye to her and allow you to give her the note intended for Betje, but you will dictate it to me and

I will write it."

"Can I at least write my own name on it? And hers?" I asked quietly.

"Yes."

He took a step closer to me and lifted my chin gently with the tips of his fingers. I looked into his eyes, and he looked into mine as a single tear rolled down my face.

"It will all be over soon, Lieve. I promise," he said, before kissing me gently and leaving me alone in my beautiful dress in the dirt stained bathroom.

EIGHT

TWO DAYS LATER ON A COOL, Sunday morning, I was standing at the doors of the estate holding Minikin tightly in my arms. She was crying because she didn't want to leave without me, but I told her that this would be my way of keeping her safe. I also told her that she would have a friend as soon as she got there and all she would have to do is give her the envelope.

I closed my eyes tightly when I heard the sound of the car tires stopping on the cobblestone driveway and willed myself to let her go.

"I'll miss you, Minnie," I said affectionately.

Even though I had spent most of my time trying to push her away, I *would* miss her brief company.

She was sobbing too hard to make any intelligible words, so instead she hugged me again and gripped the letter tightly in her hand.

"*Tot ziens*," Kerstan said, appearing behind us in the doorway, giving her a nod, and pulling me out of her arms.

The eldest grandmother exited the house and took Minikin by the arm and steered her toward the car. I watched her open the door for her and let her in before getting in behind her and firmly slamming the door shut.

I raised my hand and waived at Minnie as she looked out the back window, still sobbing, hands pressed firmly to her face.

"Why didn't you go with her?" I asked Kerstan with a sniffle.

"I only go when I bring back new merchandise. She was a gift to the other house, I guess you could say," he replied with a shrug.

Merchandise? Deep breaths, Amity. Killing him right now won't solve anything.

"Is that all we are to you?" I asked, turning to face him.

"The others, yes. You? No."

"I know I'm an investment," I replied rolling my eyes and pushing past him back into the house.

Kerstan sighed unhappily as he closed and locked the doors behind us. He had to practically run to catch up to me and when he fell instep beside me he tried to take my hand. I pulled it away and crossed my arms in front of my bare chest.

"I did what you asked of me, you know. Minikin is now safe, and you still behave like this," he said, shaking his head in frustration.

"Get used to it. Think that because you shipped her off to someone else that I'm all better? Think because I know that Betje is in a 'kinder house' it makes all of this okay? Get with it Kerstan. Shit like this is beyond wrong and you know it," I replied stopping and sticking my finger into his chest.

He looked down with a raised eyebrow, before turning his questioning gaze to me. Hushed voices suddenly filled the grand hallway we had been standing in having our "disagreement" and because of that, I knew this would result in some sort of punishment.

"What am I to do with you? You're such a

78

beautiful disaster, Lieve. I don't know how to get you to obey me without using force," he said softly.

"Then be forceful and be done with it," I replied dropping my hands to my side and preparing for whatever he felt would be appropriate enough to put me in my place.

"Not today, Lieve. I have no time for this nonsense today, but I will address this tomorrow," he said, shaking his head as he walked toward the staircase.

My body became rigid. I felt the anger boiling inside of me at being blown off and having to be made to wait, so I followed him and reached him as he got halfway near the top.

"I said do it and be done with it," I snapped, grabbing his arm to stop him.

There was a collective gasp below us. It was obvious that the others had followed to see what I was going to do, and they were probably afraid for me now.

Kerstan looked down at my hand. He didn't speak, not right away; just stood there, half turned, staring at it.

"I lied to you," he finally said.

"What?" I asked in confusion.

"I lied," he repeated, prying my fingers off of his arm. "I didn't send them to a kinder house. Betje and Minikin? They aren't any safer where they are now than when they were here.

You didn't save them *Amity*; you can't even save yourself."

I let out a scream of anger as I lunged at him. I was so furious that my vision became blurry. I tumbled forward as I knocked him back onto the staircase and began scratching at his precious face. Don't get me wrong; by no means did I fight like a bitch, I just knew how much a face like that would mean to a bastard as vain as Kerstan.

He was taken by surprise at my sudden bout of rage and tried as hard as he could to get a grip on my wrists. But each time he did, I found the strength to pull out of his grip and resume my assault. I was going to take one of his fucking eyes out before I was done.

Somehow, he managed to get his knee in between him and me, shoving it as hard as he could up into my stomach. I almost lost my footing and fell backward, but my anger wouldn't let me give up so easily. I grabbed firmly onto Kerstan's vest and used his weight to hold me in place, before I resumed my attack.

It wasn't until Xandra and two other girls pulled me off of Kerstan did I understand the severity of my actions. There were tiny red marks on his cheeks and forehead, and as he sat up he gave me the most dangerous look I had ever seen from a human being before.

A couple of grandmothers appeared, one attempting to tend to Kerstan, while the other gripped me firmly by the arm waiting for him to tell her what to do with me.

"I'm fine," he said gently shoving the one away from him.

"Take her to my room. *Now.*"

She led me up the stairs quickly and half dragged me down the hall. I was surprised at how strong she turned out to be. No way did I twist, or turn would get my arm out of her hand and as he door loomed closer and closer, I felt the blood draining from my face. I wasn't scared of Kerstan; I wasn't. I just wanted this life to be over and if it was going to be tonight, then I could only hope that it would be quickly.

NINE

REMEMBER that feeling you would get when you were sent to the principal's office in school? Sitting outside his door, hands tightly clasped together, sweat pouring down your body, and your legs nervously twitching? That's how I felt while I waited for Kerstan, only I was already *inside* his "office."

I heard the sound of his footsteps approaching the door and I took a deep, steadying breath. I would look him straight in the eye and fight my way out of this room if he offered me anything other than a quick death or freedom. I didn't see death as giving up; I saw it as finally escaping the hell I had spent the last three years in.

He pushed the doors open violently and I jumped where I sat at the edge of the bed. Kerstan had a hand on his cheek and looked absolutely infuriated with what just happened. When he stopped in front of me, he was breathing heavily, and I was barely breathing. Quickly he undid his belt and looped it around my neck, securing it almost a little too tightly before ripping my panties off and turning me over onto my stomach. He reached forward and shifted me so that I was on my knees with my ass in the air, while my arms were stuck underneath me.

"Stay just like that. If you move, I'll break your fucking neck," he seethed quietly.

After a few moments of him rifling around in a drawer, I felt the unmistakable sting of a leather belt being whipped across my bare ass. I grit my teeth and refuse to let myself cry out as he lashed me again, and again, over, and over, in a furious rage.

He was done about a minute later. I think it was exhaustion that finally caught up with him from how hard he was striking me, from how viciously I had attacked him, from my constant challenging of his authority. The belt hit the floor with a dull thud and Kerstan threw himself onto his back on the bed. I turned my face away so he wouldn't see how red my face was and how my tears stained it.

I sniffled and cleared my throat. I wanted to ask him if I could lay down too because my legs were shaking, but I didn't want to speak to him. I hated him.

I heard a phone ring and Kerstan sighed as he moved slightly on the bed. I assumed he fished it out of his pocket.

"Hallo?"

The tone of the voice on the other end of the conversation told me it was a man or a woman with a very low voice. Normally, I would have tried to listen to the conversation, but not now. Not ever again would I concern myself with matters that pertained to Kerstan Janssen.

I jumped when he raised his voice. He sat up quickly on the bed as an argument ensued with whoever was on the other end and finally ended with a mocking laugh from Kerstan, who hung up the phone mid argument.

"Bastard," he mumbled. "Would you like to know who that was?"

I didn't answer.

"Amity? Did you hear me?" he asked, leaning on his side, and putting his hand gently on the back of my head.

I still didn't answer.

"You cannot be angry with me for the discipline you received. You deserved it; I think you can agree with that," he said

with a chuckle. "Look at me please."

I took in the deepest breath in the world and held it for a moment. I knew that if I looked at him without preparing myself, so to speak, I would cry, and I just didn't want to give him the satisfaction of my tears again.

"Amity?" he pressed gently.

I let out my breath in a huff and turned my head toward him. His expression softened when he saw my melancholy eyes meet his.

"That was your final liaison. He wanted me to deliver you to him tomorrow, but I told him that you were not ready yet. I ... I apologize for shouting but he told me that I obviously wasn't doing my job and that he would seek someone else to do what he asked with you. I told him he'd have to kill me first. I won't let you go to another home; believe it or not, *I* am one of the kindest you will find in this business. I don't kill my girls if they don't see to what I ask for as many do," he said running his hand gently down the side of my face.

But would that mean that Betje and Minikin are in danger? If this sadistic bastard is one of the kindest, what the hell did he send them to?

"Betje and Minnie? Did you send them to a kind house?

Please, I need to know the truth. No more lies," I said softly.

"They are with him; the one that wants you," he replied softly. "What he will do with them or why he wanted them, I do not know, but he paid me a great deal of money for them once I told him what they meant to you." Kerstan sat up on the bed and looked back at me over his shoulder. "I don't think he'll hurt them if that is what has you concerned, but I cannot guarantee that which I do not know."

I closed my eyes tightly and buried my face into the bed. I didn't know who the fuck it was that ordered my prostitution and semi-torture, but I hope that they didn't hate Betje and Minnie as much as they hated me. Those girls had nothing to do with whatever it was that I had done to wrong this person and I just wanted to go home.

"You did not ask for Margit," Kerstan observed. "She did not mean as much to you as the other two, did she?"

"No," I replied rubbing my face with the palms of my hand, I pushed my hair back and sat back on my heels, wincing at the stinging pain of my backside. "I want to make a deal. Not re-quest, not a demand, not a barter; a deal."

"I'm intrigued," he replied as he crossed his arms in front of his chest.

"I'll do whatever you want, whenever you want, and however you want it, if it means getting out of here faster. I won't try to leave. I won't even go in the gardens without your permission. I want to know who is doing this shit to me and the only way to find out is to go to where I'm apparently meant to be," I said, glancing at him.

Kerstan gave me a triumphant look, "What else would you

require from me, if anything, before I give this consideration?"

"No more trade-offs. Any girl that speaks to me or shows some kind of interest in being my friend gets humiliated, beaten, raped, or whatever it is that you have happen to them. I don't want them to be punished because of me."

He looked away for a moment and mulled over what I had presented to him. If he didn't take this deal, he was fucking crazier than I thought. I had pretty much just laid out my plan to be the perfect little whore and he was considering it? What more could I possibly have offered? "Done."

TEN

A WEEK of playing house with Kerstan had gone by and three new girls had come into his home. I made a special point to avoid them in the event that he had lied to me at some point in our deal and would see them off.

I isolated myself from the others as well. I knew I was a serious danger to them just being around them and had asked Kerstan if I could have a room away from them. He offered to share his with me. I guess the perk about that was that he would often leave me alone in the room because he knew I gave my word to not try to escape.

So as I sat in his comfortable, large leather chair by the window smoking a cigarette, I started to make a list of people I had wronged; a list of people that I could have damaged or a list of people that I had abandoned.

Something, anything, to tell me why someone was making me feel like I had obviously made them felt at one point.

The black ink glided over line after line on the yellow papered pad as I wrote out endless possibilities, with no one standing out. Okay it was obvious why any of these names would want to see something happen to me, but why like this? And none of them even had the money for something as elaborate as having me turned into a fucking prostitute against my will of all things.

Having me shot would've been much easier and a lot quicker, but less satisfactory I guess, I thought to myself with a chuckle.

After giving the names another once over, I sighed and tossed the pad onto the floor next to where I sat. The evenings in Amsterdam were beautiful; cobalt blue skies, a dash or orange and purple as the sun faded away, and a brilliantly silver moon once the last rays of sun were gone. If it were any other time and under much different circumstances, I would have found myself loving this beautiful city.

"*Goedenavond*," Kerstan said as he entered the room.

"What does that mean?" I asked, glancing at him.

"It means 'good evening'," he replied with a smile.

I nodded and pulled my legs up onto the chair and reached for my box of cigarettes. The shit I had been going through here had turned me into one hell of a chain-smoker.

"Any new acquisitions today?" I asked, setting the lighter down on top of the pack.

"No," he replied with an amused smile. "No, today I traveled to Diemen, and I sat and watched the boats on the waterways. Tourists are interesting if you stop long enough to pay attention to them."

"You spent all day watching tourists on water boats?" I asked raising an eyebrow.

"Yes. And while I watched them I had a thought. One that I never had before," he said making his way to the bed and sitting down. He ran his hands over his face before he sighed and began to pull off his fancy shoes.

"Do you want to share your thought with me?" I asked.

"I thought of setting you free," he said quietly. "Of wiping away all debts and dealings regarding you."

I chewed my lower lip nervously waiting for him to continue. I wanted him to tell me that he was going to stick with his

thought and that I was free to go, but I wasn't going to prod him for it for fear that if he had thought this, one wrong word from me would make it go away.

"But what would I do without you, Lieve? You have challenged me like no other that has come through my doors. You cared for some of the girls; none that has come into this home has done that," he said looking at me. "So I asked myself, what I was risking by letting you leave."

"And?" I asked, taking a nervous drag from my cigarette.

"And ... I have decided to let you buy out your debt," he said slowly.

Buy out my debt? I don't even have a debt! I wanted to scream at him. I wanted to remind him that I had done nothing wrong, that I didn't do anything to deserve this, and even if I had; where was I going to get the money to pay him off?

"Guess that means I'm in for the long haul," I replied with a heavy sigh. "I don't have any money, Kerstan and I don't have anything worth shit to trade for my freedom."

"There is one thing I would consider for this," he said clearing his throat.

"Which is?"

"I very much enjoy your company, even when you are being defiant. I like how you look when you are dressed as an elegant woman, and I like the thought of having a mistress for one of my houses. With as headstrong as you are, and with as much as you care for these women, I think you would do an amazing job with this. And quite honestly, I'm tired of clashing with you. I would rather simply ask that you do it for six months and then I will grant your freedom," he said.

"But you said he was ready for me in one month like two weeks ago. How are you going to hold him off that long?" I asked staring at him.

A smile started to slowly appear on Kerstan's handsome face. A devious smile that told me that he had already thought this through, and I would probably wind up getting fucked in the process either way.

"I have more houses around Amsterdam. If you agree to this, we will leave this house in the capable hands of Saskia, and move to one of the others," he explained.

"Saskia?"

"The one who went deliver Minikin." *Oh. So that's her name.*

"And if I refuse, I go to this mystery bastard?" I asked.

Kerstan nodded and leaned past me, reaching for my cigarettes. He placed one between his lips and lit it, inhaling deeply. I never even knew he smoked. But as I watched the smoke being expelled from his full lips in rings, I somehow became overrun with fear of this person that I could be potentially sent to. Would he kill me? Torture me? Abuse me for entertainment? Pass me around?

"I'll do it."

"Good. I was hoping you would. Tomorrow morning we will leave. If you do not wish to stay in Amsterdam, we can stay at my home in Diemen." I raised an eyebrow at him. "Not a home like this one, an actual home," he added quickly.

I nodded and turned my attention back to the night sky. My last night sky over Amsterdam and sighed. I was conflicted. On the one hand this was a good thing; on the other hand, I didn't know what I would have to do to keep him happy as a mistress.

"What happens if I fuck up?" I asked.

Kerstan exhaled the smoke that he had stolen from the cigarette before answering, "Then you will be immediately sent to him."

"And if I won't go?"

"Then I'll have no choice but to make you my first," he replied.

"Your first what?"

"Casualty."

Oh.

I crushed what was left of my cigarette into the ashtray and got up from the chair. I climbed onto Kerstan's bed and undid the neatly made blankets, pulling one up to my chin. Turning onto my side, I looked at the night sky again wondering if I would somehow run into Betje or Minnie without having to run into the instigator of this whole fucking mess.

I closed my eyes and listened to Kerstan undo his belt. I heard him pull his pants off and I heard him undo his vest before pulling it off. His shirt would be next and then he would climb into the bed with me.

It was odd really. I knew the sounds of his clothing being removed and we had only fucked the one time. I knew his touch like no others even though it had been mostly been used as punishment.

"May I?" he asked laying down and hover his arm over me.

I nodded as he thanked me and let his arm wrap gently around my waist. Another odd feeling took over me as I hoped he would slide his hand under my shirt or maybe into my shorts and start to fondle me. Instead I was met with the steady breathing as he quickly fell asleep.

I closed my eyes and wondered what the fates possibly could have in store for me with a man who was hired to break me down and make me subservient. A man who rented women out to be used by men and women. A man who had no morals, not a real sympathetic bone in his body. A man who only offered me what he had because he knew I was as stubborn as he was. A man who held my life in his hands and ignited my desires with his simplest touch.

As I found myself drifting to sleep, I decided that Lieve would die that night. When I woke up the next day, I *would* be Amity Crane again. Fun loving, man crushing, mega bitch, Amity Crane.

I would find my friends.

I would free them.

Or I would die trying.

THE BAD GIRL

BLURB

I was sent away from Amity because she was my friend.

Kerstan knew that to weaken her, to break her, he would have to get rid of anything good around her.

I was traded away to live with a cruel man in a cruel house and work for his clients.

Luuk was my new owner and he made me miss home. He made me miss Amity; he even made me miss Kerstan.

See, while Kerstan was usually cruel more with his words than his hands, Luuk took great pleasure in seeing us bruised, swollen, or otherwise sexually traumatized.

Being in the house has begun to change me.

You should know me by the name of Betje.

Amity called me Wendeline, my real name.

I'm becoming sour and I'm starting to want to break free.

I want to go home.

I want to go back to Amity.

And I will do *anything* I can to get out of this house.

PROLOGUE

THE FAKE SMILE I had plastered on my face for the past two hours was starting to wear me down. I stood in the window like I had been instructed to do and I would give my little peep show to the small crowds or single parties that would gather outside my glass box without revealing anything that must be paid for.

I hated having those greedy, lustful eyes on me day after day, night after night, but this was the best bargain I could strike in my new home. To be put on display but not to be touched unless

I wished it.

A small piece of good fortune granted to me by my new owner. But certain things bothered me. If I had been traded, would I never be able to pay my family's debt to Kerstan? Did he get the money for my standing in the window being a sexual display? Did he get the money on the nights I would have sexual encounters when I knew I needed the money to pay for my – their debts?

A tap on the window stole my thoughts as I looked at the young man who was standing outside the window. It was *him;* my new owner and he didn't look too pleased that I had lost my smile or stopped showcasing myself. I immediately manifested the "sincere" smile and began to move seductively in my small space.

Luuk was not a kind man and knowing that his was unhappy with me right now, made me wish that I was still in Kerstan's home. At least he never punished us too severely. Except for Lieve, for some reason he took out a lot of our errors on her and I remember days where she would walk with her head held high into the rooms even though her eyes told us she was in pain. Kerstan didn't care for Lieve as a person and we knew it.

Oddly though by the time I was traded it

seemed like he was starting to become haunted with thoughts of her. He and Luuk had argued quite a bit about her when he brought me to him and they both left very angry. I, of course, had to endure the punishment of Luuk's anger. I wasn't able to walk for three days.

Yes. I would say that I definitely prefer Kerstan.

I turned around as I ran my hands up and down my body, spinning slowly in a circle. Twice I did this to get the attention of passersby and when I attempted the third turn, the door that held me into my glass confinement opened and Luuk yanked me out.

"I'm sorry," I said frantically. Tears sprang to my eyes and I was filled with fear. I hadn't made an error in weeks because I feared his punishments so much.

"Don't be sorry," he said quietly. "I needed to remove you from the window for a few moments."

Luuk; the foreigner who lived in the Netherlands under a Dutch name escaping from something we knew nothing about and knew better than to ask of.

My response was a nod as he led me into one of the backrooms. I sat down in the chair he told me to sit in as he began to pace back and forth in front of me. Periodic glances at the open door where I had been encased in made me curious. Was something going to happen that he didn't want me to see? He took me out of the windows but not the other girls. Yes; whatever this was, was directed at me and I wanted to know now more than ever what it was.

I shifted a little in the chair so that I could look out into the busy Amsterdam dusk without Luuk noticing. I watched as he walked toward the door and stood in front of it, hands on either side and watching intently.

"Have I displeased you?" I asked timidly.

"Did I tell you to speak?" he asked sharply, glancing back at me.

Finally after some more inspection of the outside world, he closed the door to my box and told me that I was done for the day. He told me that he was going to take me back to the house and that he would give me tomorrow as a rest day. I hadn't had a rest day in ten days and I was actually taken back by his small generous gesture. Unlike Kerstan though, I knew that any generousness coming from Luuk was always met with an even bigger take.

ONE

WE ARRIVED in Luuk's home no less than an hour later. The only reason it took so long was because he had his driver move very slowly and circle certain city blocks. I was convinced that entire painfully, long ride that he was going to strangle me and have his driver dump the body.

Leaving the house with Luuk and no one else usually meant that you were used up and either being set free or killed. The only reason you knew which was which, was because he would subject you to what I called a mental deconstruction so that you live in a semi-permanent fearful state that if you so much as thought of the house or him, he would kill you. That was a two week rigorous process. If he was going to have you killed (which he rarely did himself) he would just ask you to go for a drive with him. Refusal would be the only reason Luuk would get his hands dirty and it would always be out of a fit of rage. Like a young child throwing a deadly temper tantrum at not getting what they wanted.

He pushed the front doors to his manor open and signaled for me to follow. *Where else am I going to go,* I thought miserably.

Minikin greeted us as closely to the door as she dared. It was a bold move on her part, even though she was still at least twenty feet away. She had her hands clasped in front of her and she was looking at me with relief washed all over her face. I nodded as I followed Luuk past her. She knew I was still alive and I knew that would offer her *some* comfort.

We came to the main staircase, Luuk and I, and climbed it to the third floor. This was the floor that belonged solely to him and even though Kerstan seemed to be much more prosperous than him, he had more material things and a bigger home. When we finally reached the door to his room he turned around and faced me.

"You will not be spending the night with me. I do not wish you to come into my room, but this is the only place that we will have some modicum of privacy. Tell me why you think I pulled you out of work so early," he said, crossing his arms over his chest.

"I don't know, Luuk," I replied after a few moments of thoughtful silence.

He dropped his arms and looked down for a moment. It almost seemed as if what he knew what he was going to say was going to cut me like the deepest wound. It seemed like he actually gave a sliver of a damn as to how terribly this would hurt me.

"Betje, I have received word from Kerstan's house," he said slowly.

It was my turn to cross my arms over my chest. I began to tap my foot impatiently while he scuffed his against the carpet. Any *word* that would come from Kerstan would be about Lieve and I missed her desperately.

"What was the word, Luuk?" I asked with a curious impatience.

He looked up at me sharply. I should have

known better than to ask questions, because he didn't like having to answer to anyone. *I owe you nothing,* he told us when we came into his house, *and you owe me your freedom until your debts are paid off. Then I will decide what to do with you.*

"I'm sorry," I mumbled looking down. *But tell me what you know or I might scream,* I finished to myself.

He cleared his throat and shoved his hands into his pockets, "What I'm going to say will be very hard for you to hear, but I will not allow you to take a break from working off your debt. I want you to understand that before I tell you."

I nodded. My heart started to sink; almost as if a sudden anchor had been released from deep within and was dragging it down to a place where I would never feel again.

"Amity is dead."

I stood there and stared at Luuk. I felt sick and dizzy all at the same time as the words resounded in my mind over and over.

Amity is dead.

"How did it happen?" I asked my voice barely above a whisper.

"I don't know. I only know that Amity is dead. That is all that I received from Kerstan in the way of information. Since I know that you loved each other, I wanted to tell you. You can rejoin the other girls downstairs now," he said, turning and disappearing into his room.

I watched his door slam shut in my face and I stood there. I couldn't find it inside of myself to think anymore, let alone move. How was it possible that Amity was dead? She was the smartest of us all and she could sometimes wrap Kerstan around her finger. It was true that they hated each other fiercely and she challenged his authority every chance she could, but I could tell that Kerstan loved her in a twisted way. He couldn't have done this, could he?

Kerstan and Amity were locked in a constant struggle. He would send her out to work and she would come back with a bag full of money each time, but it would always be short. I remember one time when he asked her why there was money missing, she simply smiled at him and pulled a pack of cigarettes of out her bra and lit one.

"A girl has to have some kind of perks to keep working," she had said with a smirk.

Kerstan smacked her across the face for it and she simply threw the cigarette at his feet and stomped it out with her heel. I watched the tears well in her eyes as she held her head up and left the room.

With as much as I hate to say it, it was as if she had been so used to him smacking her and mistreating her that it didn't seem to bother her anymore.

I envied her for that. She was used to the abuse and she still defied him. She was stronger than I had ever hoped to be and now this? It didn't seem right.

I stood there for another twenty minutes before I finally found it within myself to go down to the common room. Minikin had been standing at the bottom of the staircase impatiently waiting for me.

How was I going to tell her what Luuk had just told me? How was I going to tell her that the one person that tried so desperately to protect her couldn't protect herself when it mattered?

TWO

IT WAS the next day and I still hadn't told Minikin. I hadn't eaten since Luuk told me and I slept like shit. She could tell that something was obviously wrong, but she didn't ask. Famke (former Tilly of Great Britain, the beauty with the caramel colored skin, hazel green eyes, and wild curly black hair) approached us at breakfast and sat down across from us.

"Something's wrong, Betje. It's obvious. Did Luuk hurt you last night?" she asked curiously.

"Not physically," I replied truthfully.

I liked Famke; she was this house's version of

Amity. She didn't take shit from Luuk and always stood up for us when she felt as if though we were being threatened. Of course she suffered horrible punishments for it, but like Amity, she kept a smile on her face and her head held high.

"What did the bastard say to you, love?" she asked quietly.

I glanced at Minnie for a moment. She had a spoonful of oatmeal hovering in front of her open mouth, waiting for me to answer Famke.

"I ... don't want to talk about it," I replied pushing my bowl away. I didn't even know why I had taken it because I wasn't hungry.

"Stay home today then. If he tries to make you go to work, you come find me and I'll set him straight," she said reaching across the table and giving my hand a squeeze, before grabbing her bowl and moving down the table. Famke made it a morning ritual to check on all the girls to make sure that we were all okay.

"She makes me miss Lieve," Minikin said setting her spoon back into her bowl.

"Me too," I whispered.

"*Goedemorgen dames*," Luuk said entering the room.

Everyone except for me and Famke greeted him back.

"I have an announcement to make," he said drumming his fingers along the top of his chair at the head of the table. "Who here was given to me by Kerstan?"

Please don't do this, I prayed silently as I raised my hand. Minnie raised her hand as did a new girl that must've pissed off Kerstan after I was traded because I didn't recognize her.

"The three of you knew Amity – Lieve?" he corrected himself staring at us in turn. We all nodded and Minnie looked at him curiously.

"Were you close to her?" he continued.

"No," the new girl responded. Luuk responded by waving her out of the room.

"I was," Minnie replied. "So was Betje."

"Come with me," he said to Minnie. "Betje already knows." "Luuk let me come with her," I pleaded.

"Stay here," he replied coldly as he held out an arm to Minnie. I watched desperately as he walked out of the room with her.

I buried my face into my hands and waited. Famke got up from the chair she had moved down too and came over to me.

"I'll go out there. The worst he can do is hit me," she said reassuringly as she hurried out of the room.

But no sooner had she opened the door and stepped out did

I hear the most heartbreaking wail in the world.

He told her. And she was by herself when he did it.

Famke came back into the room with Minnie half collapsed in her arms crying hysterically. My heart broke seeing her like that and I met Famke just inside the doors. She handed Minikin to me and called Luuk a bastard for not letting me be with her when he told her.

His response was a smirk.

"Amity was a bitch that needed to be broken and when push came to shove, she crumbled," he replied.

"I'm going to town," Famke suddenly said, pushing past him aggressively on her way out the door.

"Did I say you could?" he asked loudly.

"I don't need your permission, Luuk. I'll spread my legs, fuck a few people along the way, and bring money back for you, but I *am* going to town," she replied through grit teeth.

Luuk stared at her angrily and she glared right back at him. It was the most intense standoff I had ever seen where words were not needed.

"Go," he finally said waiving her off.

Famke glanced at me and gave me a nod before she left. Minnie was laid against me sobbing uncontrollably as the rest of the girls in the room looked at us. They'd never understand the heartbreak that we both shared so I didn't care if they wanted to stare.

"Enjoying the show?" I snapped.

Maybe I cared a little. But it wasn't for me, it was for Minikin. She was overcome with grief and she had an audience to witness it.

"Yes."

I whipped around in Luuk's direction. He was standing at his chair again, watching us with a smirk sitting on his lips. I can't exactly say what took hold of me at that moment. I only really remember grabbing everything that I could get my hands on from the elaborate table settings and throwing them at him, hoping that I would hit him with something.

The sound of the sickening crack as I finally connected against his face with one of the glasses was deafening. The silence that followed as he stumbled was deadly. I watched numbly, as a trickle of blood appeared above his left eye and began to lazily roll down the side of his face.

"Give her to me," one of the girls, who I think had been renamed Ilse, said urgently as she reached for Minnie. She gently pried her out of my arms and took her back with her to the group of girls who were staring at Luuk in shock.

"Get out," he said in quiet, seething tone. The rest of the girls quickly scrambled and ran from the room through the back doors except for Ilse. She handed Minnie to one of her friends and came over to take me out of the room too, but Luuk shook his head slowly.

"Out," he said to her again. "The bitch stays."

"But Luuk —" Ilse started to protest and he cut her off with a sharp look. "You can take her place if you'd like," he said in a sinister tone.

Ilse wrung her hands for a moment. She looked at me with tears in her eyes before she hugged me, kissed my forehead, and ran out of the room. *Just make sure Minikin is safe from here on out,* I thought silently after her.

When we were left in the dining room alone, I got to my feet and faced Luuk. I had a modicum of courage swelling inside of me; something I had obviously taken from Amity and Famke. I would take whatever punishment he would dole out to me as long as Minnie was safe and left alone.

I watched him as he wiped the blood off of his face and chuckle. His hands moved down to his belt buckle and he undid it, pulling the leather strap loose.

"Come here," he said pointing to a spot directly in front of him.

I lifted my chin a little higher, stood up a little straighter, and walked with purposeful long strides to where Luuk had directed. I was afraid, terribly afraid, but I would be damned if I would let it show.

"Do you know that I could kill you for this?" he asked calmly.

I nodded and waited.

"And do you think I should?" he prompted.

"What you do to me is of no consequence anymore. My best friend is dead and I have no resolve to live," I replied bravely.

"So, perhaps I should just have Minikin go through another round of what went through with Kerstan before she was given to me?" he asked, a disgusting smirk crossing his face.

"No!" I closed my eyes for a moment and took

a breath to steady myself. "No. Please. Leave Minikin out of this. I was the one that attacked you, I deserved to be punished."

"I meant what I said when I called you a bitch," Luuk said conversationally. "Take your panties off and bend over the table, Betje."

"What are you going to do to me?" I asked nervously eyeing him and pulling my underwear off.

"Break you," he replied simply.

I closed my eyes tightly as I bent over the table and gripped the edges. I grunted in the next breath as he brought the belt down as hard as he could over my bare ass. Tears stung my eyes because my pride was wounded.

Luuk spent the next ten minutes whipping me repeatedly until he decided he was tired and I had been punished enough.

I'd give anything to go back to Kerstan, I thought as I struggled to reach down for my panties and cried out in pain as the delicate silk touched my burning skin.

THREE

ONE FULL WEEK passed before the pain finally went away. Minnie and Ilse spent their time taking care of me and my welts, which was quite humiliating, but I'm sure that was part of the punishment.

In the seven days I struggled to be able to sit again, Famke was gone. She hadn't come back and I wondered if she had absconded and why she didn't at least take Minnie with her. One of Ilse's friends entered the room and came over to my bed. She leaned over and whispered something to Ilse in their language and handed her a piece of paper.

Ilse looked around before she unfolded the paper and read its contents. I saw her look of surprise coupled with a gasp of shock. When she was done she quickly folded the note and slid it underneath the mattress.

"I'll burn that later," she said quietly. "Eva brought news. While she was out today with her clients, she came across a man that spoke of his distaste for Luuk. She said she approached him as if she were going to proposition him, but the man brushed her off and told her that he would not fuck a whore from this house.

He also said that she would be better pressed to work for him." Ilse gave me a knowing smile.

"Kerstan?" I asked in shock.

"She described him as tan, green eyes, and somewhat long black hair, and absolutely beautiful."

Yeah, that's Kerstan alright. The devil in disguise himself.

"Where did she see him?" I asked desperately.

"She did not write it down. She said that when she realized he was of another house, she quickly left his side because she fears he will tell Luuk."

"Did she Famke?" I asked.

"She did not say, so I assume she did not," Ilse said sadly.

"Goddammit, where did she go?" I wondered out loud more to myself than them.

Famke

FINALLY IN THE *heart of Amsterdam, Famke,* I thought grimly to myself. I had spent the first five days in hiding. I didn't want to be caught and sent back to Luuk until what I had set out to do was done, then I would return of my own volition and accept whatever he decided needed to be done with me.

I hated Luuk more than I hated anything in the world and I hated that he made picking on Betje and Minikin into a fucking game because he didn't like Kerstan. They were like little boys constantly trying to prove that their whores were better than the others, while we put in all the work and didn't get shit for it.

I reached the fourth and largest house that lined the outskirts of the Red Light District and knocked on the door. My game plan was to pass myself off as a girl looking for work and see what I could find. I wanted to speak to this Kerstan person about how Amity died so that Betje and Minikin could find some kind of solace in this fuck hole of a situation we were all in. They didn't deserve to be there at such young ages. I had fucked up and got too far into drugs and gambling and so yes; I owed a debt and I would work it off, but I would not allow them to be used any longer than they had to be.

I waited patiently. A few minutes passed before an elderly woman opened the door and I immediately thought I was in the wrong place.

"I'm sorry. I was looking for work and possibly a place to live, but I think I'm in the wrong place," I said turning to leave.

"What kind of work?" she asked in a surprisingly strong voice.

"Um, well I'm really good with my hands among other things."

She stared at me through narrowed eyes for a moment before telling me to wait where I was and closing the door in my face. I shrugged and turned my back to the door reasoning to myself that I would wait five minutes and move on. Three minutes later the door opened again and I looked over my shoulder.

Wow. The man that was leaning in the door-frame was gorgeous to say the least and the way his lips curved as he smiled was enough to make my panties wet.

"You were looking to speak to me?" he asked in a Dutch accent.

"Are you the owner here?"

"I am."

"My name is Famke," I said turning to face him fully. "I'm looking for a place to stay and possibly to work for the roof over my head and meals. Are you taking anyone new?"

He chuckled and turned to his side, leaning his back against the doorframe and putting his hands into his pants pocket. He was wearing a black vest with a dark blue long sleeve button down shirt underneath. The sleeves had been rolled up to above his elbows and as I looked down I noticed his immaculately shiny black shoes.

"What do you think you would be doing for me here,

Famke?" he asked, glancing at me with an amused look.

"Whatever you required of me," I replied.

He nodded in approval and motioned for me to come into his home. I followed him silently, jumping when the door slammed shut, and kept my wits about me. When I had first been taken to Luuk, I had been drugged no more than two steps inside and woke up naked and shackled in a dark room.

As we walked past another elderly woman he said something to her that I didn't understand. She nodded and walked quickly away.

"Do you belong to another house? Will I have to barter for you?" he asked me as we walked down the long hallway toward a heavy wooden door.

"No."

"Good," he said pulling it open and stepping in. I walked in curiously behind him and found myself in a large room with half naked girls sitting around on beds chatting excitedly.

"Looks like we've got a new girl!" the leggy blonde with the Scandinavian accent called out. I nervously looked at the man who was standing next to me. He shook his head in disapproval at the outburst, but nothing more.

"This is Famke; she will be joining our house," he said nodding at me.

"Careful girlie! If Kerstan likes you, he'll fuck you instead of sending you out to work and then you'll be stuck here forever like me," a brunette with big blue eyes and an American accent called out.

Kerstan? I found him? Finally!

"Lieve, why must you always do this?" he asked in exasperation.

"Because I like to piss you off," she replied simply.

"Lieve?" I asked curiously stepping closer to her. "Your name sounds very familiar to me."

"Lieve is my hooker name. Call me Amity," she said lighting a cigarette.

FOUR

"YOU'RE NOT DEAD?" I breathed in disbelief.

"Obviously not," she replied dryly. "Why is that the new rumor? Killed me off already, did you?" she asked turning her attention to Kerstan who was now staring at me questioningly.

"Why did you believe her dead?" he asked.

But her hair isn't blonde. Not completely anymore. This can't be the girl I'm looking for, I thought shaking my head.

"Famke," Kerstan said sternly. "Did you lie to me? Do you belong to another house?"

I put a hand to my chest and tried to steady

my breathing. "My owner's name is Luuk; he told Betje and Minikin that Amity was dead."

Amity sat up immediately at the sound of her friends' names. She got to her feet and came over to me and gripped my arms firmly.

"Are they okay? You're in the same house with them? Oh God, tell me they're okay!"

Tears slid down my face. Luuk was more of a monster than I thought he was. He took great pleasure in wearing us down physically but moving on to mental degradation was way worse than any smack or belt lash.

"Luuk?" Kerstan cut in with a half-smile on his face. "Defecting are you? I won't turn you away if you'd like to stay. That bastard owes me and he knows it."

"Why would he say you were dead?" I wondered quietly to myself. "Minikin – I swear I've heard her heartbroken cries every time I've closed my eyes since."

Amity put her arms around me and took me over to her cot. She balanced her cigarette between her lips as she pulled off the sheet on the bed next to her and wrapped it around me.

"You've got to find a way to let them know I'm alive," she said looking at Kerstan.

"Do I?" he asked raising his eyebrows.

"Kerstan, for fuck's sakes! Those two never did anything to you. They were *my* friends so you sent them away to Mindfuck Land and now you're going to let them keep thinking I'm dead? Come on! Where the fuck is your decency as a human being?" Amity yelled at him.

"I'm trying very hard to control my anger right now, Lieve," he said quietly. "I ask that you lower your voice and have respect or it'll be at least a month before you can walk again."

Amity took a deep breath and got off of the bed. She went over to Kerstan and sat next to him quietly choosing her next words.

"I'll do the thing you've been dying for me to do. With you only if you just please let them know that I'm alive," she mumbled looking at the floor.

Kerstan looked at Amity, then he looked at me. "Does Luuk know you're here?"

"No. I told him I was going to town; that was seven days ago."

"You told him or asked his permission?" he asked.

"I don't ask Luuk's permission for anything. I *told* him," I replied coldly.

"I think we've found the Amity Crane of *that*

house," Kerstan replied rolling his eyes. His statement was followed by a sigh. Amity kept her eyes on him as he contemplated what he was going to do.

"I don't like that you lied to me," he said looking at me. "I don't tolerate things like that and because of that, my answer is no. I will not allow word to go back to Betje and Minikin that you're alive, Lieve."

Her mouth dropped open. I think that whatever it was that she was offering to do with him or for him would gain his favor, but he rejected it because of me.

"Go back to your house. That's your punishment," Kerstan said getting to his feet.

"Fine!" Amity yelled. She ran over to a closet that sat along the far wall and began to pull out clothes.

I watched her silently as did the rest of Kerstan's women as she pulled on a pair of denim shorts, a t-shirt, and fished around the bottom of the closet before pulling out a pair of simple, flat black shoes and sat on the floor while she slid them on. When she was done she got to her feet and came back over to where I was sitting.

"Let's go," she said in a determined voice,

yanking me off of the bed. I looked at Kerstan nervously as we walked past him toward the door.

"Stop right there," he said in a low, menacing tone. "You are *not* going to that house, Lieve."

"The hell I'm not! You won't tell them that I'm okay, then I'll tell them myself!" she yelled at him.

"Amity, you will not go to that house. You aren't ready for that just yet," Kerstan said coming over to us. "Famke will go back alone and you will stay here with me," he said prying us apart.

Amity reached for Kerstan's hand and pulled it off of my arm and opened the door. She gently pushed me through and slammed the door closed behind us.

"Run or we'll never make it to the front door," she said urgently as she broke into a sprint.

I'd like to think that if we hadn't spent the time glancing over our shoulders we would have made it. I'd like to think that Amity didn't suffer to terribly when Kerstan easily caught up to us and slammed her face into the door, knocking her out cold. I'd like to think that he wouldn't tell Luuk that I had been there and that I was trying to desperately defect.

I'd like to think a lot of good things about him, but as I walked home with him following closely in his chauffer driven car, in tears, and terrified, I soon learned that maybe Kerstan was worse than Luuk after all.

FIVE

Betje

ON THE NINTH evening that Famke was missing, we were all sitting in the dining room eating dinner. I sat with Minikin to my left and Ilse to my right. Ever since we were told that Amity was dead and Famke disappeared, I refused to let either one of them out of my sight.

The doorbell rang reverberating throughout the house and Luuk glanced at one of his servants and waived them out of the room to answer it. I glanced down at my plate still full with vegetables, mashed potatoes, and thin cuts of pork shoulder on it unable to find my appetite. If Luuk had noticed, he hadn't said anything.

I sighed and placed my fork gently down on the plate and looked at the other girls. They were all eating quietly and I couldn't help but feel like we were in some kind of twisted convent because of the strict silence during meals rule he had.

"Luuk," the servant said frantically as she entered the room. (Luuk's servants were older whores of his that could never figure out what to do with their lives once their debts were worked off.) "Luuk, you must come quickly."

He glanced up at her looking completely annoyed that someone was speaking during a meal and got up from his seat. He used his cloth napkin to wipe his mouth before he dropped it onto the table and followed her out.

A few moments later there was an eruption of raised, angry voices coming from the main hall. We all jumped in surprise and looked at each other wondering who would be brave enough to peek and see what was happening.

"I'll do it," Ilse finally said.

"Be careful," I whispered as she got up and ran toward the door. She opened it slightly and peeked out before she turned around and waved me over.

"Look," she said moving slightly so that I could look into the brightly lit hallway.

"Oh my God," I breathed.

It was Famke; she was back, but she wasn't alone. She was standing there in bitter tears, with her head down as Luuk argued with a man I couldn't quite make out. I can't say that I was thinking clearly when I ran out into the hallway toward Famke. I just knew that she was scared and I wanted to be there for her.

But the closer I got the clearer the man came into view and my quick paces slowed to a screeching halt when his eyes wandered over to me. The slow smile that spread across his lips was so familiar and the way his eyes pierced into me made me feel unsteady on my feet.

Before either of us could say anything to each other, Famke let out a rush of frantic words, "Amity's not dead! She's not! I saw her! She's still alive!"

The snapping sound that followed hit me like a shot in the heart. I watched as Kerstan moved his hands away from Famke's neck and watched her body collapse onto the ground between him and Luuk.

"Keep your whores away from my house, or the next time it will be you," Kerstan warned Luuk.

I watched as he callously nudged Famke's lifeless body with his shoe before he turned his eyes back up toward me.

"You and Minikin are to stay away from my home and Lieve, do you understand? Don't send anymore spies to me. You both had your chance and you screwed up. Now you have to deal with it," he said evenly.

My lips trembled as I looked Kerstan in the eyes. I wanted so desperately to attack him for what he did to Famke and I wanted to attack him for sending us away when we did nothing wrong. But instead I turned toward Luuk and kept my eyes off of Famke so I wouldn't lose my nerve.

"May I please go outside and get some fresh air?" I asked in a shaky voice.

He nodded. Without hesitation Luuk permitted me the one thing that he had denied us all unless we were stepping outside to get fresh air, fuck someone, and bring money back in.

"Thank you," I whispered as I walked past them both and out the front door.

I collapsed onto the stairs and began to sob. This was all wrong; Famke shouldn't be dead. Kerstan shouldn't be here and Minikin didn't deserve this life of sexual slavery.

A pair of strong hands grabbed me by the shoulders and I looked up through a veil of tears to see Kerstan's most trusted Grandmother pulling me to my feet.

"Come quickly, Betje. We came for you and Minikin; where is she?" the old woman asked me.

"She's still inside!" I replied frantically.

"Then she must stay," she said pushing me toward Kerstan's waiting car. She opened the backdoor and ushered me inside instructing me to lie down while she hid me beneath a blanket.

My heart was racing. I was terrified of what would happened if I was discovered and even more terrified of leaving Minnie behind, but if Amity was still alive, I knew that she would come in person to retrieve her and Luuk wouldn't be able to deny her. Not only was she beautiful, but she was cunning with her words and would be able to strike a bargain for Minnie.

The car door opened and closed.

"Drive," Kerstan's voice said. "I'm sorry about your friend Betje, but she deserved it for her transgression. I will take you back to Lieve and somehow I'll get Minikin back too. But I want you to know that I don't do this for either of the two of you. I do this for Lieve."

I closed my eyes as the car drove away from the House of Luuk back to the House of Kerstan. I felt myself become less afraid because I knew that Amity was at the other end of the drive. I let out a sigh as I fell asleep the rest of the way back.

"WAKE UP, TROUBLEMAKER," a voice gently said.

My eyelids fluttered and I turned on my side. The voice sounded so familiar but if it was true then it would be a dream walking through my nightmare.

"Wendeline, my little German brat," the voice said affectionately brushing a hand over my hair. "Wake up."

I groaned as I turned on my side and forced my eyes open. I blinked a few times to get them to focus and I turned my head slightly.

The kindest face, the brightest blue eyes, and the most genuine smile greeted me. It was her. It was Amity; her hair was no longer completely blonde, but it was *her*.

I sat up and wrapped my arms tightly around her, crying into her chest. She laughed kindly and hugged me close. Neither of us said anything further, we just held each other until I was done crying like a lost child.

"I'm sorry about your friend."

I pulled away from Amity slightly and saw Kerstan suddenly standing behind her, his arms crossed over his chest.

"You killed her!" I shrieked jumping up from the bed and trying to claw at him. Amity, however, gripped me around the waist and pulled me back down onto the bed.

"It was either her or you, Wendeline," she said quietly. "Kerstan didn't have a choice."

My head started to spin and my temples started to ache. What the fuck was going on? Why was she defending him? Had that much changed since we had been given away?

"We have to get Minnie out of there as soon as possible," she said to Kerstan.

"I know," he replied with a heavy sigh. "I

obviously can't go back to do it and I won't let you go. If we send her back he'll kill her," he said nodding at me.

"What the fuck is going on?" I asked rubbing my temples. "It almost sounds like the two of you are working together when I know you can't stand the sight of one another."

Amity cleared her throat and glanced up at Kerstan. He nodded and she turned her attention back to me.

"We've come to an understanding; almost a stalemate to be able to co-exist. Part of my deal in cooperating with the new set of rules for me is that he gets you and Minikin back. So far, I can see he's holding up his end of the bargain. One down, one to go."

I looked at the large bump on her forehead and raised an eyebrow, "So he still gets to knock you around? That sounds like a shit deal to me."

She laughed and put a hand to tenderly to the bump, "Still working out some of the kinks. That hasn't happened in a long time and I think someone regressed back to their old selves for a minute."

Kerstan chuckled slightly before he walked toward the door. "I'll have one of the grandmothers take her to my room. She'll rest better there. Amity, you come with me. We have to things to discuss." I looked at Amity and she smiled at me before she left the room with Kerstan.

A moment later the same elderly woman who had helped me escape from Luuk's house entered the room. She gently, but firmly wrapped an arm around my waist and helped me off of the bed. We went down the hallway back to a grand staircase and up to a private floor. It was kind of weird how there were barely any other doors on this floor yet so many on the others.

Amity

"THAT WAS PRETTY risky of you; to go into his house yourself and try to get them back," I said quietly as I walked next to Kerstan.

He nodded without so much as a glance toward me and made his way to the formal parlor. I had only been in there once before, when we sat down and negotiated our new terms. We had spent nearly all night arguing, because he didn't want to get Betje and Minnie. Of course, when I told him that Lieve would die an instant death and Amity Crane would be back in full force, he conceded.

Kerstan put his hand on the elaborate gold door handle when we reached the parlor and hesitated for a moment.

"Are you sure that you want to get Minikin back? What I did

... It has put a mark on this house," he said uneasily.

"Don't worry. If any ninjas come flying through the windows, I'll be sure to fuck them back out," I replied breezily, reaching for the door knob.

"This isn't a game, Lieve," he shot back angrily. "You still have the will of a child in many, many things and you don't understand what can possibly happen now. To my girls, to you, to my grandmothers. Nothing will happen to me; that would be result in too much trouble for Luuk, but the rest of you are now targets."

"Listen if it bothers you that much, then close the doors until we figure it out. There *are* other brothels in town you know," I said pulling the door open.

"No. He would expect that and I don't want to lose business. You're do to be out and working soon too. You know how much money you make me," he replied closing the doors firmly behind us and locking them.

I rolled my eyes but didn't say anything. Apparently the world would come to an end if he allowed me to tighten up. Or any of the girls for that matter. I sometimes wondered how he would feel if he was being used for money he didn't get to keep. I also wondered how he felt if whenever he was asked by one of us how much closer we were to paying off our debts, he would just smirk and dismiss it.

I had a theory about Kerstan and our debts. Even though I was pretty sure he had an immaculate book keeping system, I think it was the part of the psychological hold on us that made him feel so powerful. I mean honestly, where would we go once we left? What would we do? A resume with "red light entertainer" wouldn't be impressive to anyone and we'd get judged for it. It would be instant and never ending and we'd probably come back to his house begging to be let back in until we aged into grandmother's for the next person that would take over. It was an ongoing vicious cycle in the red light district; when one proprietor, I guess you could call him, aged out or moved on, there was another one ready and waiting to take his place with the eagerness of a salivating jackal.

But what became of them when they aged out or quit? The house owners? The men that conducted the sexual fantasies of so many others, what did they end up doing? Surely they wouldn't have to want for anything, because I was damn sure that they kept all if not a huge percentage of the money that we made for them.

I guess the only way to know for sure is to ask.

"Can I ask you something?" I said, sitting in his big leather chair in front of his desk.

"If the question was if you could have my chair, I think you've already answered that," he replied shaking his head.

"No, not that. I was ... Well, I guess I was just wondering. I think it's safe to say that our lives are pretty much over after this, but what about you? What do you go on to do?" I asked, pulling my legs onto the chair and hugging them close to my chest.

"What do you mean?" he asked, sitting in the

smaller leather chair across from me and crossing one of his legs over the other.

"I doubt that you'd ever quit this lifestyle. Are you a lifer?"

A knowing smile spread across his face. He finally understood what I was getting at, now the question was, would he actually answer me truthfully.

"I've been thinking about how to get Minikin out of there," he said conversationally, completely disregarding my question.

I rolled my eyes and sighed. I don't know why I expected an answer. Kerstan wasn't built that way.

"And?" I asked tiredly.

"Well, you know how I told you that I couldn't send you to Luuk? I think that's our best shot at this point. I only said it in front of Betje, because I'm sure he's had a few things to say about the great Lieve and she wouldn't be able to deal with my sending you. Truthfully speaking, if you want Minikin back, you're going to have to go get her."

"Fine. Just tell me where to go and when I can leave," I said getting to my feet.

"Wait," he said seriously, holding a hand up. "I don't think you're mentally ready for this yet.

I'm going to have to figure out how to prepare you for this, Lieve."

"For the last goddamn time; my fucking name is Amity and you *promised* you'd call me that when we were alone," I replied letting my breath out impatiently.

Kerstan got to his feet and came over to where I was standing looking like an angrily little girl. Okay, so maybe I was behaving like a spoiled brat, but the perk of going to get Minnie alone would be that he wouldn't be able to make me hold up most of the bargain we'd struck. *He* didn't do all the dirty work. Now it would be up to me.

SEVEN

Luuk

I WAS STANDING on the balcony of my bedroom looking out into the dark pink skyline. How Kerstan had made it past the front gate to get onto my property was something that I would make everyone answer to. I wasn't given notice that he would be here and he had not only seriously injured my most expensive whore, he had trespassed into my home like it was my own. I know that it seemed as if though Famke were dead, but he didn't kill her. The angle at which he dislocated her shoulder made the others believe that she was dead and I let them think so while she recovered in my room.

To them Famke was dead and Kerstan was a monster, which is exactly what I wanted. They would do anything they could to avenge their fallen "sister" and I would put their anger and hurt to good use.

"Luuk?" Famke asked in a tired voice from my bed.

"What?" I barked.

"Nothing," she replied in a small voice.

I turned slightly and glanced at her over my shoulder. She was sitting up now and looking longingly at the bedroom door. I knew she wanted to leave and I knew she wanted to let the other girls know she was okay, but that would foil my plan.

Famke would just have to stay dead a little while longer.

I sighed and looked out over the skyline again. Somewhere out there was the real reason I was in Amsterdam. Somewhere out there was the *only* reason I had taken on this facade of owing a house. *Somewhere ...*

"I wasn't always this angry," I grumbled to the dusk sky.

"I didn't believe that you could be," she replied softly.

I huffed and gripped the railing tightly. I wondered how long Kerstan was going to keep testing my patience. I wondered how long he would keep from me the one thing we had bargained so furiously on. I wondered a lot of things lately, but I wondered most of all if forgiveness was possible.

I know it sounds odd to think of, because what could I possibly need forgiveness on? Many things. Many, many things that haven't yet been brought to light.

"Luuk, when will I be allowed to leave your room?" Famke asked quietly.

"When I say you can. For now you need to heal and I need time to think," I replied.

"Think of what?" she asked curiously.

"Many, many things."

Amity

I WAS GETTING sick and tired of Kerstan speaking in code so I decided to stay in his parlor when he left. I decided that if I did some snooping, I'd figure out what the fuck was going on as opposed to waiting and finding out. I hated surprises with an unbridled passion. I had good reason though, the last time I was "surprised" I wound up out on the street and being dragged to Amsterdam.

I can't say that my life completely sucked. I mean because I was such a good lay, I was able to get some perks out of my pimp and he hadn't hit me in a really long time since before Famke showed up. Honestly, I think that Kerstan was starting to develop a little crush on me ever since I fucked him but it only happened that one time and that was the "thing" he kept asking me to do for favors. He told me that he had had many whores in his house and only fucked a few and I was definitely his favorite.

Because I knew I had this power over him, I kept my pussy away from him at all costs. I knew that eventually I'd let him in again, but only when I had no other option to get what I wanted.

As I watched him leave the room I thought of how I hadn't really gone out to make money lately and I kind of understood why he needed me to go out and work. The other girls brought money into the house in droves, but what seven of them made in one night full of men, I could make with one man.

I spent the next half an hour destroying the room trying to find something, anything, that told me about our debts but I found nothing. It took me another hour to set the room back exactly as it was and fifteen minutes after that to realize that I still hadn't seen Wendeline after she had been sent to his room.

I didn't know where Kerstan had been going when he left, but I suddenly got a bad feeling in the pit of my stomach and ran out of the room, leaving the door wide open and running as quickly as I could up the main staircase toward Kerstan's floor.

When I reached his floor, I was out of breath which was kind of embarrassing considering the endurance I had for other things. The embarrassment gave way instantly to curiosity when I heard the sounds of quiet moaning coming from his slightly open door.

I approached quietly and looked through the slit between the door and the doorway and saw

Wendeline naked, face down on the bed, and ass in the air. I raised an eyebrow and opened the door a little more and almost gasped when I saw that Kerstan was fucking her gently. He was *fucking Wendeline.*

His pants were around his ankles and he still had his hoity toity vest and shirt on, but the way he was moving and the sounds that were coming from her.

Motherfucker, I thought with a twinge of jealousy. He had told me that after me he didn't want to fuck any of the other girls in the house or anyone else, and here he was taking advantage of one of the girls I loved the most.

His hands gripped her hips tightly as he moved in and out of her. She turned her face slightly and locked eyes with me, tears streaming down her face, silently begging me to get him to stop.

"What the fuck is going on in here?" I yelled, shoving the door wide open.

Kerstan stopped moving and turned to look at me, a glimmer of laughter on his handsome face. He shoved Wendeline off of his dick and reached down for his underwear and pants, pulling them up but not securing them yet. I watched him walk over to the nightstand and grab a tissue, wiping himself clean of her. After he tossed the used tissue into the garbage can, he pulled them all the way up and zipped his pants closed.

"Get out of my room, Betje," he said to her.

She quickly scrambled to her feet and ran naked past me, crying quietly.

I slammed the door closed behind her and put my hands on my hips, turning to face him.

"Well? What the fuck was that?" I asked.

"Precisely that. You won't let me touch you so I guess I could say that she reminds me of you in a way. She was laying here asleep when I came in and I couldn't help myself," he replied simply with a shrug.

"Stay away from her or I *am out of here*," I seethed through clenched teeth. "She's been through fucking enough without having to worry about being your fuck toy."

"And where will you go?" he asked in amusement. "Home?

Do you have a home anymore, Lieve?"

Oh great; here comes Mr. Cruel Fucker, I thought to myself rolling my eyes at the ceiling.

"Cut the shit, Kerstan. You know damn well that if I have too, I'll defect to another house," I said impatiently tapping my foot on the carpeted floor. "Better yet, maybe I'll talk the girls into tearing this place apart so we can see where we stand with your damn debt collection."

"Do what you think is right, Amity," he said in an even tone. "And I will do what I think is right as well. Now, I don't have time for this. I have to figure out how to get Minikin back so I

can get you to spread your legs for me again."
Prince Charming, eat your heart out.

"I'll give you until tomorrow afternoon to think of something. If you haven't by then, then I'll go to Luuk's house, kick in

the door, and fucking drag her out myself."

EIGHT

Minikin

I DON'T KNOW how the other girls had convinced Luuk to let me stay in the house. After Betje was taken away and Famke died, I had such little faith in anything anymore, that I was too sad to work. Now I just lay around in the dormitories hoping that he would either kill me or just let me be. I didn't want to work anymore. Everything that I loved was being taken or destroyed and I just didn't have the will to do anything about it.

This must be what Lieve feels like. But how is she strong enough to push through it like it doesn't hurt her? How can these things not crush her? Does she not feel like a normal person?

"Minnie?" a voice said softly into the room.

I didn't roll onto my side to see who it was. I knew it was Ilse because of her voice, but I just didn't have it in me to turn and face her.

"I promised Betje that if anything happened to her, that I would look after you. Sit up; I've brought you dinner," she said as her footsteps made their way toward the bed.

"I'm not hungry," I half said into my pillow.

"I don't care. You haven't eaten for a couple of days. You need some nourishment for your body. You can lay down again after, but for now you must eat," she said setting a tray down on her lap. I felt her hands as she gave my leg a gentle tug.

With a sigh, I turned onto my back and used my hands to help myself sit up. Ilse smiled softly at me. She used a hand to gently push away the stray hair in my face, before she picked up the tray and moved up the bed, closer to where I sat. I let my arms fall limply between my legs as she spooned up some kind of white lumpy substance and began to feed me. I knew how proud she was, so for her to be doing this must mean that she really cared about me in some way.

"I'm sorry," I said quietly between spoonfuls.

"For what?" she asked, digging the spoon back into the yellow plastic bowl and wiping the excess off on the rim.

"For acting the way that I am. I just miss my friends. I miss Lieve, I miss Betje, I miss Famke, even though I didn't really know her."

"You have me though," she said with a kind smile.

Yes, but for how long? I wondered to myself. I didn't dare speak the words out loud though. It was pretty damn clear that Luuk liked friendships in his house considerably less than Kerstan. At least *he* would tolerate it. With the exception of Lieve, who seemed to be his personal project.

Ilse stayed for another ten minutes to finish feeding me before she left with the tray full of dirty bowls, spoons, and an empty glass.

I lay my head down again on the pillow and turned my back to the door once more.

Something had to give soon, or I knew I

would antagonize Luuk to the point of his taking me on a car ride.

One that I knew I would never come back from.

NINE

Amity

YOU'RE A FUCKING GENIUS KID, I thought to myself with a sly grin. I had convinced Kerstan to let me go out into the gardens that night. I think he was so quick to comply because he saw how viciously angry I was at what he had done to Wendeline.

Of course by now he must've figured out that I had left the property. I mean the sun was fucking coming up already.

To be honest, I only had one fear with what I

had done; that he would hurt Wendeline to get back at me for leaving. I was coming back, but I was coming back with Minnie. I refused to leave her in that new place by herself. I knew that she was a sweet girl and she had probably made a friend or two, but she belonged in *my* house.

I sighed as I reached one of the main roads in town and put my hands on my hips. It would've helped if I knew where I was going, but I'm sure if I said Luuk's name enough, I would either run into one of his girls or clients. Either way, I'd get to where I was going eventually.

"Lieve?"

I turned around apprehensively and saw a man that looked vaguely familiar. He was giving me a charming smile with his brilliantly white teeth. I could almost swear if this were a cartoon you would hear the *ding* noise from the whiteness of them. His light brown eyes looked into mine and he ran a hand through his dark blonde hair.

"Hi," I replied curiously, still trying to place him.

"Are you still, um ... You know," he said cutting his eyes nervously around us.

Must be a former client.

"Yes."

"You don't remember me, do you? I was your first … Um…

You know," he said giving me a lopsided grin.

I rolled my eyes.

"My first paying fuck?" I asked loudly.

An older couple that was walking by turned quickly and eyed us both distastefully before they continued walking. His face turned red with embarrassment as he mumbled a goodbye and started to walk away.

"Wait!" I called out. I walked quickly to catch up to him and put a hand on his arm to stop him. "Sorry. I can be a bit of a bitch sometimes."

"I've noticed," he replied darkly.

"Listen, do you know anyone named Luuk? Does what Kerstan does? Maybe you've paid for some company from his house?" I asked.

He looked at me sternly for a moment, like he didn't like to be reminded that he paid for prostitutes, before he sighed loudly and nodded.

"So where do I go to find him?" I asked excitedly.

"Why would you want to?"

"What's your name?" I asked impatiently.

"Joris."

"Okay Joris, so this Luuk guy? He's holding one of my friends hostage. I know, I know; how can a whore be a hostage, right? She doesn't want to be there and I'm going to get her back, so if you could be a super awesome guy and just tell me how I get there, I won't have to keep yelling out that you paid me for sex once upon a time."

His eyes widened at that prospect and he lowered his voice telling me which way I would have to go to get to Luuk's place.

"Thanks Joris! Stop by Kerstan's sometime and ask for me!"

I replied cheerfully as I walked down the street I had started on.

I gave a glance over my shoulder and saw him walking away shaking his head. He wasn't a bad looking guy, kinda cute actually, so I wouldn't mind giving him a go again. He would be my last great conquest before I ran away with Betje and Minnie.

I hadn't exactly thought about how I'd do that last part, but I wasn't going to stay in Amsterdam any longer than I fucking had to. Debts cleared or not, we were going to leave.

After about an hour of walking, I stopped to eat in a charming bakery almost on the edge of the downtown area. I was hungry, thirsty, and my legs hurt. I didn't have much money left after this little feast, but I figured a cab shouldn't cost me too much because I should be close to where Luuk kept himself and his girls.

I finished my coffee cake and my coffee fifteen minutes after I got to the bakery. With as much as I would've loved to just sit there and blend in with the normal folk, I knew that there just wasn't time for it. The longer I wanted to sit there and pretend to be something I wasn't, the longer Minnie had to be stuck in that place being subjected to God knows what.

After I threw my trash in the receptacles, I walked over to the counter and asked the young girl behind the glass if she wouldn't mind too terribly calling a cab for me, to which she nodded and bounced away from view.

Twenty minutes later, the cab pulled up outside. I wanted to reach into the front seat and grab the man by his shirt collar and shake him for taking so long, but instead I hopped into the backseat. After I got comfortable, I told him which way I needed to go. When he asked for an address, I shook my head and told him to just go the way I was telling him.

Ten euro later, he pulled up in front of a large, gated property and I got out. I wrapped my arms around myself as I made my way up the driveway toward the front door.

When I reached the large wooden front doors, I raised a fist to knock when I heard my name. My *real* name.

"Amity Crane!" a man called out.

I immediately looked around and saw that I was by myself where I stood with no one in sight, so I did what any normal person would do; I looked up.

And there he sat with that beautiful smile. Those deep dimples that set whenever he grinned the way he was grinning now shown even from where he sat.

On a window sill, on the third floor, with an arm draped casually over his leg, and a smile on his face.

That was the last thing I remembered before the world went black and I collapsed into a heap on the gravel.

TEN

Minikin

THERE WAS a sudden commotion in the house and I wasn't sure why. I had been rustled out of my sleep over it because of the girls running back and forth in the hallways whispering excitedly to each other.

It took me a moment to clear the grogginess from my mind as I pushed myself up to a seated position. I yawned before I swung my legs over the side of the cot and got to my feet. I stretched my arms over my head and leaned back a little, cracking any bones that had tightened while I was sleeping before I made my way to the door.

Ilse greeted me with big eyes and a huge smile.

"You're going to be so happy! Follow me! Quickly," she exclaimed as she grabbed me by the arm and yanked me into the hallway.

"What's going on?" I asked impatiently as I let her drag me down the hallway, past the main staircase, and into the main dining room.

"Look!" she whispered as she pushed the other girls out of the way and let me see into the slit between the doors.

At first I wasn't sure what I was supposed to be seeing. There was a girl in the room with long brown hair, but nothing else, so it couldn't have been her.

At least, that's what I believed until I heard a wrenching sob come from the room. I knew that sound; it was the sound that I had heard the night that Betje was sent away.

"Lieve?" I asked, my voice shaking.

The blonde hair turned toward the door and wiped tears angrily away from her face.

"This isn't a fucking freak show! You can all

stop staring at me like I don't belong!" she yelled, throwing a plate toward the door.

"Lieve!" I exclaimed happily, shoving the doors open. I cut my foot on one of the pieces of the broken plate, but I was so overjoyed at that moment, that I didn't let the pain bother me.

"Minnie?" she asked, suddenly looking so pitiful that my heart broke.

"Yes; it's me," I confirmed falling to my knees in front of her chair.

Lieve put her arms around me and began to cry harder than I had ever heard from her before. I let my head rest on her lap as she brushed her hand over my hair, saying how sorry she was and that she knew that this was where she truly belonged now. She said that this was a set up and that she had fallen for it. She said that she had already bargained for my release and that I would be going back to Betje. She also said that I would never see her again but begged me not to worry about her.

I pulled away from her at that and grabbed a cloth napkin off of the table. I used it wipe her tears away.

"Lieve, you know I would never leave you here. This place ...

It's much worse than being in Kerstan's," I said lowering my voice.

"You don't understand," she said with a chuckle and fresh tears.

"What is there to understand? When I leave you leave with me. That is the bargain or we both stay," I replied firmly.

"Luuk isn't who you think he is," she said with a sniffle. "I need you to leave and trust that I'll be okay."

She pushed me gently but firmly away from her. She nodded toward the door and when I refused to get up, she reached down and yanked me to my feet. She put her hand tightly around my arm and dragged me toward the door. She gave me a quick hug, a small kiss on the lips, and a gentle shove through the open doors, before she pulled them closed tightly and used a chair to lock herself in.

ELEVEN

Betje

IT HAD BEEN three months since Minnie had come back and still no signs of Lieve. Kerstan wouldn't speak of her and if you dared to ask him where she was, he would correct you with a stern slap to the mouth.

I was proud to say that it still didn't stop me from asking from time to time.

I had tried everything I could to pry information out of him. Asking questions incessantly, offering him sex for any piece of information, which he took, but never complied with a word about her whereabouts.

"I don't fucking understand this!" I yelled in frustration. I was sitting on her bed and I became angrier, colder as the days rolled by without her.

Was she dead? Was she hurt? Was she ever going to be set free?

"I've told you to stop worrying about her. Even though she seemed scared, she kind of seemed at peace with everything," Minikin said from her bed at the end of the room.

"That's bullshit! I can't believe you just left her there!" I seethed at her. "She went through so much to get us both back and you just let her. She loved you, Minnie."

"I know. And I love her too, but getting slapped around or fucked by Kerstan for information obviously isn't getting you anywhere," she retorted. "If you know Lieve as well as you think you do, you know she'll be okay. You also know that she'll find

her way back if that's what she truly wants to do!"

I shook my head in disbelief. These months without Amity had made me cold and bitter.

Nothing would be able to fix me if I couldn't see her just one more time.

I was sick and tired of being the good girl of this goddamn brothel. I was sick and tired of being the push over and I was fucking sick and tired of being the one that was always sit around and just *wait*.

Unfortunately, Kerstan had already warned that anyone that left without his knowledge or permission, he would make sure didn't come back. To his house or *any* house.

"*Goedemiddag dames,*" he said tiredly, suddenly appearing in the doorway. Everyone in the room except for me answered him.

"Betje, I've been informed of what you've been saying," he said turning his attention to me. I watched him slide his hands into his pockets as he liked to do when he was ready to "correct" one of us.

I glared at him, "And?"

"And I think it's best if you leave well enough alone," he replied with a heavy sigh.

"You know, with as much as you hate to admit this to yourself, I know you cared about Amity too," I said to him.

He chuckled and rubbed his chin thoughtfully before replying.

"No. I cared about how much money she brought in for me. I cared about how she was willing to let me fuck her when I wanted and I cared about how she showed the most subtle hint of jealousy when I had you bent over in my bed. But her? I didn't care about *her*. Just what she could do for me," he explained with a shrug.

"I never thought that even you could be such a heartless bastard," I said shaking my head in disbelief.

"Lieve is where she belongs and that's all that matters," he said sharply.

"All that matters," I repeated huffily under my breath. Little did he know that I would not accept that she was away from us when it was so clear that she had come to get us. She had come to bring us home and I swore to myself in that moment that I would do the same for her. Amity wouldn't be abandoned. I wouldn't allow it.

BITTERSWEET HEROINE

BLURB

I never wanted to go back to the Red Light District.

Once I had successfully paid off my debt to Kerstan, I thought I was done.

But something has been bothering me; rumors of an American girl being shoved from house to house, being used, treated worse than any of us have ever been.

I know it's none of my business but I feel like I won't truly be able to put the Red Light District behind me if I don't find some way to help her. I'll go back to the house I belonged to and gather the information I need to find her.

My name is Valentina; call me Danique.

I'm the self-appointed Patron Saint of Abused

Whores and I'll save Amity Crane by any means necessary.

PROLOGUE

MY NAME IS VALENTINA. I am the only woman who worked for Kerstan and successfully paid off my debt. I want to tell you what it's like to recover from being used for money. I want to tell you that everything gets better and I want to tell you that eventually you'll be okay, but I can't. It never gets better and you never get over it. You're left feeling used, unworthy, and lost.

My interests no longer lie in the Red Light District. At least they didn't until I heard rumors of what was happening in his home. An American girl who was basically stolen to work for him, by a man she knew but always was kept away from. A new house owner of no less than three years who treats his girls horribly. The rumor is that his treatment of the girls is all that he wishes upon her, but doesn't have the heart to inflict himself. That's why he had Kerstan take her. That's why she became the best at what she did.

I don't want to say that I'm a hero by any means, but I want to save her. Even though I don't know her, I feel that the best way to destroy what these vile men have put her through would be to save her. *Saint Valentina; Patron saint of abused whores,* I think to myself with an amused smile.

As I sit in my small bedroom in my even smaller apartment, I dress myself in my black lingerie. Kerstan's favorite when he used to send me out and I remember that now I am no longer Valentina, I'm Danique again; the best whore that the Red Light District had ever seen until the American girl, Lieve.

As I pulled on my striped white and black fitted shirt, my black short flare skirt, and my favorite pair of black high heels, I know that to undo Kerstan and save the American girl, I have to go back into what I left.

I have to immerse myself back into the Red Light District.

The only way to really save myself once and for all is to save her too.

I take one last look around my small bedroom before I turn off the light and leave my apartment. The best place to start this would be the one place I had managed to escape.

I have to start at Kerstan's.

ONE

I KNOCKED on the door and waited. One of the elderly women that Kerstan used as decoys to his business would open the door, I'd ask to see him, and stay outside. If I walked back into that house voluntarily it would be like asking him to take me back and I refused to give him the ability to have power over me again.

As expected, one of the grandmothers opened the door and greeted me in shock. *She recognizes me,* I thought with a tight smile.

"I wish to speak to Kerstan. Tell him Danique is here," I said evenly.

She nodded and opened the door slightly gesturing for me to come in. I shook my head firmly and sat down on the steps. I heard her close the door firmly and the sound of her hurried footsteps.

It couldn't have been more than five minutes before the door opened again and Kerstan stepped out.

"Could this be a dream?" he asked with a chuckle as he descended the steps and stood in front of me.

"I'm more of a nightmare," I replied with a smirk.

"Danique. What brings you back to my humble home?" he inquired, crossing his arms over his chest.

"I've been hearing rumors," I said conversationally. I glanced up at him, but he didn't reply, he only raised an eyebrow in curiosity. "There's a girl, an American that used to be here in this house. I'm wondering where she is now."

I already knew the answer, I just didn't know how to get to where I was going and I needed him to give me the information.

"Where have you heard rumors that I would

have an American working for me?" he asked evenly.

"I run into old clients from time to time," I replied with a shrug. "I hear this Lieve is the new Danique and I'm dying to meet the girl who has taken on my legacy and surpassed it."

"Jealousy doesn't look good on you," he said with a grin.

"You mistake curiosity for jealousy, Kerstan," I replied shaking my head. "You never were very empathetic though."

He threw his head back and laughed. I always did enjoy his laugh because it was a rare thing to hear. I smiled in amusement and waited for him to compose himself.

"She isn't here. She hasn't been for quite some time."

"I know that," I replied rolling my eyes. "I'm here because I want to know where to find her."

Kerstan eyed me for a moment before he shook his head. "You should know that I won't tell you. However, if you'd like to work for me again, I have a place for you."

I got to my feet and looked into his eyes, "Never again will I *ever* ask to work for you. I paid off my debts and I'm a free woman now. But if you change your mind on letting me know where the American is, you know where I live."

I turned and started to walk away when he called out my name. Not the name he gave me, but my actual name. "Valentina! Wait!"

With a sigh, I stopped walking and turned slightly to glance at him. Coming toward me, he rubbed the back of his neck uneasily as he stopped a few feet away from me.

"This isn't any of your business. I don't understand your sudden interest in Amity—Lieve, but you should know that this is something completely different from your situation."

"Her name is Amity?" I ask curiously. "Amity what?"

"Leave it alone," he said finally losing his gentlemanly composure and sticking a finger in my face. When I opened my mouth to protest, he turned on his heel and stalked back to the front doors of his house, walked inside, and slammed them behind him.

Crossing my arms over my chest I looked up at the windows. So there was something different about this American, Amity. This wasn't a business deal; this was a vendetta. The perfect revenge designed to humiliate her and take away any dignity she had left.

TWO

I DECIDED to walk around downtown Amsterdam instead of going home right away. Kerstan's warning played over and over in my mind. He wanted me to "leave it alone" but I was a naturally curious person which was how I ended up in his house. He also knew that I was never one to really do what he said so I was left wondering how I was going to figure out this mystery. How was I going to get to this American girl without knowing where to start?

With a sigh, I sat on a bench in a pleasant

park that overlooked the Rhine River and weighed my options.

The first was that I could knock on Kerstan's door every day for the rest of my life hoping he'd answer. The second was that I could ask around and see if anyone knew where the Amity girl was. And the last option, the one I wanted the most to avoid, was to strike a bargain with Kerstan. My services for the information I was looking for.

Redemption is such a bitch, I thought to myself wryly.

I decided I would find a hotel in the area for the evening. Tomorrow, I would go back to Kerstan with my decision. Whatever that may be.

THREE

Amity

IT TOOK DAYS, but I finally stopped crying. I was sitting in a room underneath the house alone and above me I could hear the other girls walking around, the front door opening from time to time. I would hear Luuk's voice raise in anger causing the tears to spring to my eyes again. I fought them back every time; I refused to give him any further feeling of worth at the expense of myself. Instead I stayed where he put me after I stupidly made my way here and I stubbornly wouldn't come out.

Luuk told me that he would leave the door unlocked for me and that when I was ready to join the other girls, he would welcome me back upstairs into his home. *Luuk,* I thought bitterly to myself, *where the fuck did you come up with that name?*

"Luuk" as he called himself was a ghost from my past. I understood now why the things were happening to me that were. I understood now that all hope was pretty much lost on any kind of redemption. The feeling of absolute shock and dismay when I looked up as he called out my name. The realization of who had been doing this to me and why Kerstan had once told me that I wasn't ready for this encounter yet made more sense to me than anything in the world.

Luuk was actually Smith Lennox; Theo's younger brother and we have a very bitter history.

Smith never thought I was good enough for Theo and Theo always thought that Smith thought I was perfect enough for *him.* I never thought of Smith as anything other than my true love's brother; he never thought of me as anything other than a meaningless whore, which he had told me I was quite a few times, prompting endless fights with Theo. It got worse when I slipped one night and drunkenly had sex with

Smith and with as much as I hate to readmit this to myself, I know that Theo chose me over his family and that only wound up sending Smith to a dark place of resentment and apparently vengeance.

A soft tap at the door distracted me from my thoughts. I glanced over as it began to open slowly and Famke peeked her head timidly in. "Amity?"

"Still here," I confirmed softly.

"Can I come in?" she asked.

"Yes, but be careful not to push the door closed all the way or we're both fucked until *Luuk* decides to let us out," I said emphasizing his name angrily.

I watched her as she came into the dimly lit room, pulling a chair in behind her, and closing the door only slightly. Famke brought her chair over and sat it across from me, smiling as she sat. I raised an eyebrow at her and crossed my arms over my chest waiting to find out what she wanted. I knew she was only trying to be kind, hell the girl had traveled half of Amsterdam to find me, but I wasn't in the position to start making friends now. Especially knowing that Minnie was upstairs somewhere being left to the sadistic whims of that piece of shit.

"You know him, don't you?" she asked, after a few moments of thoughtful silence.

I nodded.

"How?"

"That's none of your business," I said, shaking my head, "I'm sorry, I don't want to be a bitch to you because I know what you went through to make Betje feel better, but I can't keep doing this. I can't keep trying to befriend you girls only to have you traded off, raped, beaten, or killed. I have enough on my conscience already and he's just another reminder of where I went wrong."

My words stung her, I could tell by the look on her face. I would be as verbally abusive to them as I had to be to be able to keep them all safe regardless of how they would think of me in the end. Unfortunately my priorities had switched now. Instead of coming to break Minikin out, I spent my days in this room wondering what I could possibly give Smith to let her go.

"Tell me something," Smith said entering the room and giving Famke such a dangerous look that she left me alone with him. "How many years did you think it was my brother that did this to you? How many years did you fuck random men and women for money and just know that it had to be him even if you never uttered the words out loud?"

The smug look on his face as he took the seat across from me was enough to make me want to punch him in the face. Unfortunately for me, once I came to realize who had sold me to Kerstan, I had lost all of my inner strength. The fire that burned inside of me night after night, man after woman after man, seemed to be snuffed out immediately.

"I never suspected Theo," I replied quietly.

"Liar!" he yelled, slamming his fist on the table. "You always suspected him, because of how horribly you hurt him. It's okay to finally admit it, Amity. If it makes it easier on you, he stopped loving you when you whored around with me. I might even think it's safe to say that he never truly loved you."

I felt the hot tears stream down my cheeks and wiped them away quickly before they had a chance to fall completely. I sniffled and took a deep breath. I wanted desperately to tell him how wrong he was and how in love Theo and I were and how much I loved him still. I wanted to tell him that no matter how many men and women I had been forced to fuck for money, that I still had dreams of being in Theo's arms one day. But I knew he wouldn't believe me and it would be a waste of breath because a small, terrifying thought floated in the back of my mind. What if he really *doesn't* love me anymore?

Valentina

IT HAD TAKEN A FEW DAYS, but I finally wound up getting a lead. Apparently some of my former customers told me that an American girl had been seen in the home of Luuk from time to time. There were whispers about her from the girls that took them as clients, which was a strict no-no in our line of work.

But it intrigued me, nonetheless and lead me

to find out where exactly this Luuk's home was. Because I was so good at what I used to do, my last former client that I had run across gave me the information for a simple favor; to let him jerk off while looking at my bare breasts.

It was a small price to pay for what I was looking for and at least he wouldn't have to touch me. Once I had what I needed, I covered myself up and left him to clean up his mess in the small room we had rented in the hotel above a takeout restaurant.

The day had quickly disappeared and I was now walking through a darkened night on the way to Luuk's. I didn't want to waste any time in freeing this girl. I wanted to get my own life back and didn't feel that I could fully do so without her help.

With tired legs but a damn determined will, I reached Luuk's sprawling home. I would dare say that it was impressive and larger than Kerstan's. Hell, I'd have to let Kerstan know again someday that he had some serious competition, but for now I walked up to the door and knocked loudly.

When there was no response I knocked again. When there was still no response, I kicked the door as hard as I could. That's when I heard the footsteps approaching quickly. The door swung open and a young, irritated man stood in the doorway giving me an angry look.

"This isn't a round the clock business that I run. Come back when the sun is out," he barked.

"I'm not here to make a purchase," I replied with a small smile.

His demeanor changed almost immediately as he stepped out of the doorway and walked around me slowly. I knew what he was doing; he was looking for scars, marks, anything that would make me unattractive to potential buyers.

"What debt do you have?" he asked once he had made his full circle around me.

"Only the debt to myself."

"Everyone that comes to my door has a debt," he said with a smirk. "I can always use another strong girl, but I need to know your debt first."

Not yet, Luuk. First I want to have some fun, I thought my smile widening a little.

"I will owe you a debt when I leave your house," I started carefully. "What I will ask of you is to speak to Lieve."

A look of intrigue washed over his face as he went back to his doorway. He leaned in the frame, crossing his arms over his chest, and raised an eyebrow.

"Why?"

"My business is my own."

"Not when the whore you seek is mine," he shot back, his face becoming angry again.

I scoffed and crossed my arms over my chest. I knew that the only way I would able to get near her would be to make a bargain. And when you had been in the Red Light District as I had, you knew there was only one bargain to be made.

"I'll work for you. For one month, in exchange that I be roomed with the American," I said. "Done."

FIVE

Amity

"MY NAME IS AMITY CRANE. I'm twenty three years old and I'm an American. My name is not Lieve. I'm not nineteen years old and I'm not Dutch."

I repeated the words over and over to myself trying to emblazon it into my mind. I was starting to feel myself mentally breaking under Smith's watchful eye and I knew that once he had me where he wanted me, he'd probably kill me.

He had already told me that he had no intention of letting me leave Amsterdam and he assured me that I would never see Theo again.

A tear trickled down my face as I looked bravely into the mirror and repeated the words quietly to myself.

"My name is Amity Crane. My name is Amity Crane..."

"Who are you talking to?" a curious, accented voice asked behind me.

I turned around and saw a beautiful blonde woman smiling at me. I wiped the tears away quickly and glared at her.

"What do you want?" I asked.

"Did you say your name is Amity?" she asked.

"Yes."

"Then he held up his end of the bargain. My name is Valentina, but in the Red Light District, I am Danique," she said coming forward and holding a hand out toward me.

I rolled my eyes and walked away from the mirror. I could already tell this wasn't anything I wanted a part of. This would be the same song being sung every time I made a friend, only this time, it would be at Luuk's mercy and not Kerstan's.

"I don't care who you are. I don't want to be

your friend. It doesn't matter who *I* am, just stay away from me," I replied miserably.

"I understand," she said, sitting on one of the two empty beds in my room. I watched her cross one of her long legs over the other, as she leaned back on her hands and spoke. "I used to be just like you when I first started. Kerstan would do the same thing to me; if I made a friend he would immediately find a way to send them off or get rid of them. If I worked hard for him and kept my thoughts to myself, he would give me days where I wouldn't have to go out. I'd get to stay with him and please him at his whim. This Luuk that I've heard of? I can tell this is something personal and I don't think I like the way this will end, so I came to help you get out of here. I can get you back to Kerstan and then you'll have to figure out the rest from there."

I raised an eyebrow at Kerstan's name. Actually it was more at the mention of how Kerstan had treated Valentina. *Almost exactly like me.*

"So, is that something he does with all of his best girls?" I asked, trying to mask the disappointment in my voice.

Before she could answer, Ilse ran into my

room and looked at me, her eyes wide with excitement.

"Lieve, you have to come with me! Now!" she said holding out a hand to me.

"What's wrong?" I asked, moving forward and taking her hand.

"Kerstan has just arrived," she whispered excitedly.

What? Why is he here?

I let my curiosity make my hand close around hers tightly as we left the room. Ilse told me that he was in the main room with

Luuk and that they were talking angrily with one another.

"Over what?" I asked. "You."

Kerstan

I SAT FACING Luuk with one hand on the table and the other draped over the back of the chair. Something about seeing Danique again reminded me how much I wanted Lieve back and I didn't plan on leaving without her. I knew this would be difficult and I knew that Luuk wanted his pound of flesh, but I decided that he would have to take it from me and not her.

"I won't give her back to you. You knew the deal from the very beginning. You train her to be the whore that I knew she's been her entire life, then you give her to me for her final humiliations," Luuk said simply.

I wondered what he truly had against Lieve. He never did tell me the whole story because I was so intrigued by the fucking plan he had that it never dawned on me to ask more questions than I already had. My eyes wandered toward the ceiling as Luuk kept giving me his reasons that Lieve was now "property" and I tuned him out. Besides the fact that I wasn't listening to his nonsense anymore, I concentrated on the door behind me. I heard faint footsteps stop just behind it and whispers that went silent as soon as they approached.

I wondered if it was her. I wondered if Danique had made it here safely. I wondered what about Lieve had drawn her back into this and I wondered if Luuk could tell she had a motive. Then I chuckled as the whispers started again softly.

"Do you not have control over your own home?" I finally asked, cutting off his incessant rambling.

"What are you talking about?" he asked curiously.

I smirked at him and shook my head as I got

to my feet and walked to the door. I put my hand on the doorknob once I reached it and slowly tilted my hand to look through the sliver of space between the door and the frame. Once I confirmed my suspicions, I pulled the door wide open and watched as three women fell on top of each other. Each had a black leather collar around her neck and had on white panties only.

Blonde, brunette, and a fading color. Let's see if I can sort them out.

I gripped the blonde first by the arm and pulled her to her feet. She gave me a big half grin and I shook my head, laughing as I positioned her next to me.

"You were always too curious for your own good, Danique," I said.

"And it's always gotten me what I wanted, hasn't it?" she asked her grin widening.

"Yes. It has."

I leaned down and reached for the small brunette girl and pulled her too up by her arm. I looked up her up and down carefully as she kept her eyes to the floor.

"Very nice," I said with an approving nod. "Your name?" "Ilse," she replied softly.

"Give her here; you have enough," Danique

said pulling her out of my grip. I rolled my eyes and let the girl go. She was beautiful and would probably make me a great sum of money, but it was true. I had more than enough whores and wealth than I knew what to do with these days.

"Up you go," I said to the last girl, securing her arm in my hand. She hesitated for a moment, turning her face away from me, before she let me pull her up unsteadily to her feet. "Look at me, Lieve," I whispered softly. I knew it was her by the profile of her face and the curves of her body, now that I could fully see it.

She shook her head and tried to pull out of my grip, but I held on, made my way around her, and stopped when I was facing her. She turned her face again so I couldn't see her face. I put my hands on her arms letting her use hers to cover herself with, and felt a single tear drop land on me. Her body shook as she struggled to keep her eyes away from my face, but I knew Lieve well enough to know it wasn't from fear. She shook as hard as she did and cried her quiet tears because she was furious with me.

"Take her and wait by the door," I said to Danique. She nodded and took Lieve from my arms, as well as Ilse from my side and turned to leave the door when a glass flew passed my head and shattered on the wall. "Is he always this childish?" I asked Ilse, who darted her eyes nervously toward Luuk.

Danique pushed Ilse out of the room and closed the door behind her. I raised an eyebrow as she quickly began to pick up the shards of broken glass before taking them to the table and dropping them on an empty plate. She sat down in the chair I had been in when I was attempting to negotiate Lieve's freedom with Luuk and spoke.

"I know I asked for one month with the American, but I've got a better deal for you. I'll stay here as long as you want, work as many hours a day as you want, fuck as many men and women as you tell me to, if you let her go now. This will be the debt I told you I would owe you," she said conversationally.

Luuk, the angry boy House Master, leaned forward to look Danique directly in the face. His eyes were so stern and evil, but she didn't falter. Not when he told her no, not when he demanded she leave his house, and not even when he grabbed a shard of the glass and made a terrible gash along the side of her beautiful face for her defiance.

SEVEN

Amity

HOLY SHIT!

I moved away from Kerstan's side and went over to Danique who was still sitting across from Smith. She had calmly taken a cloth napkin from the table and placed it against her cheek. Her heaving shoulders told me that she was in pain and when I reached her, she looked up at me with glossy eyes and a small smile.

"Have you lost your fucking mind?" Kerstan shouted.

Smith got to his feet, dropped the bloodied piece of glass on top of the table, and looked at Danique.

"You have a new face courtesy of your new friend," he said with a smirk as he walked toward the door.

"I'm so sorry," I said, my voice cracking. She held up her hand for a moment, then waved it quickly to let me know she had already forgiven me. Danique, a woman I had never met before today, had already forgiven me and I couldn't even forgive myself.

"Help me," I begged Kerstan desperately. He came over quickly and pulled the napkin away to see her face. *Oh God.* I had to turn away. Not because it was a deep cut, but because I knew it would leave a terrible scar and it didn't have to happen.

"Can you walk?" Kerstan asked her. She closed her eyes tightly for a moment, before she nodded and pushed herself to her feet. At first she was a bit unsteady, but Kerstan gripped her tightly so she wouldn't waiver any more.

"I can't do this anymore," I said more to myself. I sank to the floor and choked back my tears. I couldn't live this life anymore. I couldn't live the life that caused people around me to get hurt because of a young man's boyish tantrums. *If I hadn't fucked up my life with Theo none of this would have ever happened.*

"I need you to help me get her out of here, Amity. We have to take her back home so the grandmothers can tend to her," Kerstan said, leaning down to pull me up off of the floor.

I didn't realize how strong he really was until that moment. And with the way he held her against him and did his best to make sure I was okay too, almost made him seem *human.* But I knew this would come with a price too. There would only be one way to end this entire charade once and for all and getting to where I needed to be to end it would be damn near impossible.

I took ahold of myself, calming my emotions. I wasn't sad anymore and I wasn't desperate either. I felt what I was feeling in Camogli after I had surfaced from seeing the Christ of the Abyss statue. I felt what I was feeling when I woke up in a strange house with a strange man and had to fight to stay alive. I felt like Amity Crane; not playful, somewhat bitchy Amity. No, I was the *real* Amity. Determined, strong, and a fighter.

I was going to show Smith why Theo had

fallen in love with me. I was going to make him understand the parts of me he had never seen before and I was going to make him understand what it was like to survive; truly survive like the villa in Italy had taught me to do.

I pulled myself away from Kerstan, "Take Valentina outside. Get her in your car and take her back to your place. I'll be behind you soon."

"Not without you," he said firmly, shaking his head.

"I promise, Kerstan. I'll find my way back to you. There's something I have to do."

He looked into my eyes curiously. I'm sure he expected me to tell him my plan, but I still had to work on it.

It would probably take days, weeks, or maybe even a few months, but I would accomplish what I needed to do and I would finally be freed from the chains that held me in Amsterdam and I would take as many of the girls as I could with me.

EIGHT

Valentina

I KEPT pressure on my cut. The napkin I held against it felt wet and warm and I wondered how the hell it was possible that something like this could have happened. It should have been easy; get in, find the American, and get out. Now I wouldn't be able to work for Smith because he knew and I wouldn't be able to work for Kerstan because *he* knew as well.

I sat back against the lush leather seat in Kerstan's car as he yelled at his driver to go as quickly as he could. He sat with me in the back and pulled the napkin away again.

"Does it hurt?" he asked me.

"*Niet*," I replied, slightly shaking my head.

"Liar," he said with soft chuckle as he pressed the napkin back against the side of my face. He sighed and ran his hand back through his hair, "Why didn't you listen to me when I told you not to go? Did you really think I was going to leave her there?"

I rolled my eyes, slid away from him, and glanced out the window. "This is not about you and what you want. This is what I have to do for *myself*. I chose to help the American because I heard rumors about a House Master falling for one of his girls and I knew it was you. Who else would it be? You forget that I was one of your first workers, Kerstan. I know how soft you can be even though you portray yourself as something completely different. Have you really become this cruel, this hard?" Kerstan sighed.

"I am whatever is required of me to keep my business intact and unchallenged. I was going to stop a couple of years ago, but then Luuk, he approached me with a business offer I couldn't refuse. In return for helping him set up his own

House and getting revenge on a whore that tore his family apart, I was to get an even split of the money his girls made for him. How could I say no?"

"And the American? How do you feel about her?" I asked with a grimace. I hoped this conversation would be over soon, as I was starting to feel dizzy.

"I feel nothing about her," he shot back, giving me a stern look.

I smiled at him, a knowing smile that told him I knew better, before I leaned my head back against the seat and closed my eyes. It took another ten minutes for the feeling of nausea and dizziness to go away, but that was better than not going away ever.

I felt strong hands wrap around me moments later, and opened my eyes. I was tired and I'm sure it was due to the loss of blood, but as I looked groggily into Kerstan's face, I knew I would be somewhat safe for now. He reached into the car and pulled me up into his arms, cradled me against his chest, and used his foot to close the door as he walked toward the main doors.

As soon as he walked through the doors, there were gasps and whispers. He bellowed for any of the grandmothers and as they approached, he began speaking to them rapidly in Dutch. He told them that I was to be taken care of hand and foot on a twenty four basis. He told them to call a doctor who would come and glue my wound so that it wouldn't scar as terribly as it would with stitches.

In a matter of him being done giving them directions, he set me on my feet and one of the elderly women took me away to my own private room on the floor. One I imagined had once belonged to the American at some point.

I sighed as the grandmother laid me down on one of the two beds and told me she would be back with clothes and a warm blanket for me. I closed my eyes again, but reopened them moments later when I felt like I was being watched.

"Did you see her?"

I turned slightly on my side to get a better look at the girl with the angelic face, drawn tightly together in old anger and desperation. She had long brown hair, big brown eyes, and kept her arms crossed tightly across her chest. Her accent was not of Dutch descent, but I couldn't figure out where she was from.

"Amity? Did you see her?" she asked again, taking a few tentative steps toward the bed.

I didn't answer. Not for any reason other than I didn't know if I could trust her. Instead, I pulled the napkin away from my cut, opened and refolded it, and pressed the cleaner side down.

"Do you speak English? Do you understand or speak German. I don't speak Dutch. I understand some of it. Amity? Lieve?" she asked desperately close to tears.

"Are you a friend?" I finally inquired.

"Yes. My name here is Betje, but my real name is Wendeline. Is she okay? Is she alive?"

"She's alive," I confirmed, not wanting to say much else about how mentally broken Amity seemed to be.

"Thank God," the little German said, sitting on the bed next to me. "I miss her so much."

I watched her wring her hands as she looked at me. It seemed as if though she wanted to ask me more questions, but wasn't sure if she should.

"Out," Kerstan said entering the room. He walked over to Betje and affectionately put a hand on her shoulder. "She needs rest. You and I will talk in a moment. Wait for me in the hallway."

The German girl got to her feet and stared at

me for a moment, before she turned her eyes to Kerstan, nodded, and left the room.

"That's her best friend," he explained as he sat down where Betje was. "I hadn't been very kind to her and Lieve tried to protect her from me. I wasn't happy about it so I had some things done to her while Lieve watched then I sent her to Luuk."

"I'm not a priest," I replied in a labored voice. The numbness was starting to go away and the pain was starting to creep up on me.

"I'm aware," he said with a wry smile. "But I think that you should be aware of how I've ... evolved as a House Master since you've been gone. It'll help both of us; me if you let me talk about it and you, if you listen."

I rolled onto my other side so my back would be to him. It hurt like hell since that's the side my cut was on, but not only did I not have time for stories I had no want for them either.

He scoffed as he the bed creaked, signaling him getting to his feet.

"Eventually you'll have to listen. The doctor is on his way. Stay in this room until you feel better."

I heard his footsteps retreating as he left the room, following by the door closing.

With my eyes closed, I sighed again. I hadn't even come close to saving the American and now Luuk knew the real reason I had come to his house.

I can't save her yet. I haven't even saved myself.

NINE

Famke

THE SCREAMS WERE STARTING to haunt me. Ever since the Dutch girl had left with Kerstan, Amity had been wailing. It scared me because I didn't know what was wrong or what had been happening to her to cause it.

Luuk had locked her back into the main dining room once they had left and warned us that if we let her out or went near the door, we'd be found floating in the Amstel river. He said no one would care about a discarded whore and everyone believed him.

Everyone but me.

In the moment that Kerstan had spared my life, I learned that not all House Masters were bastards like Luuk. It made my fear of him and my want to be free clash together with my quest for freedom being the winner.

I wanted to help her, but not the way Kerstan's girl wanted to help her. I wanted to set her free, truly free, to stop the pain and anguish she had suffered in her short life. Not because I hated her, but because I could see myself in her and I didn't know if I would be able to sustain myself much longer if she was around.

Amity would be dead, I'd be in jail for the crime and we would both be away from Luuk. It was the perfect plan, I only had to figure out how to execute it.

I took a deep breath as I left my room. The other girls were asleep somehow and the halls were empty. I walked quickly to the dining room and almost stopped short when I saw the door was slightly ajar.

I looked down at my bare feet for a moment wondering how I close I could get before I was noticed. I pushed the fear of being caught out of my mind and walked toward the door again when she let out a howl.

The closer I got the more my body started to shake. The howling, the wailing; something was obviously very wrong. I walked up to the door and I pressed my face against the opening, as the dim light illuminated a small portion of the room. It took my eyes a full sweeps of the room to find her and when I did, my hand flew to my mouth.

She ... she was under the table, the chairs had been knocked out of the way, the table had been flipped on its side, and there was a group of men standing around her ... they were ... taking turns with her.

I watched as she fought wildly until two of the men restrained her while a third pushed himself onto her. Amity let out another scream as the man viciously moved in and out her until he was finished. Then another climbed on top of her, then another. And all the while Luuk was standing against the far wall, his arms crossed over his chest, as he watched Amity being gang raped by almost every client he had.

I felt myself becoming ill. I turned around and I ran from the room. Killing Amity wouldn't save her, hell it wouldn't save *me* either. This was our life now and this is what we were meant to be.

I got back to the room and I threw myself onto my bed and started to sob. Ilse came over and laid down behind me, wrapping her arm around me.

"Are they hurting her?" she asked quietly.

A heart-wrenching sob was my only response. I couldn't nod my head, it was still full of the image of what was happening to her.

"Can we help her?" she asked.

I let out another sob, feeling absolutely helpless. There was nothing anyone could do to help.

"Famke, stop crying. There's something I have to tell you. It'll help us all, but I need you to pull yourself together for me. Please?"

She pulled her arm away from me and sat up. I rolled onto my back, trying to steady my breathing, as I wiped fresh tears away.

"When Kerstan and his girl were leaving, I slipped a note to them. No one knows this, but I've been in Luuk's room. He's used me for his own personal pleasure before and I've talked to him about things. Did you know that he has a brother named Theo? Did you know that Theo and Amity were very much in love? I wrote that down and got it to Kerstan when he was leaving. If somehow he can find Theo and bring him here, maybe this will all be over. Maybe this nightmare will end and maybe we'll be able to get out of this with whatever dignity we have left."

I looked at her like she had lost her mind. Why would Kerstan want to help us? Any of us? We weren't his girls and Amity was just his fuck toy when he wanted.

"Give it time. We'll be out of here soon," she promised, before she went back to her bed and pulled her covers up over her head.

I wish I had her resolve.

Theo

I WAS STANDING in the airport asking myself for the millionth time why I had put so much stock into a random phone call.

I didn't even know who the guy was and it was kind of hard for me to understand what he wanted, but what I did understand were two words that made my heart beat erratically; Amity Crane. As soon as he said her name and Amsterdam, I was booking the first flight flying over.

For all of her faults, I still loved her. I had every intention of making her my wife before she went temporarily nuts and partied her way into my little brother's bed, but I loved her so much that I was willing to forgive that.

I just wanted her back. I felt a part of me die off when she left. She said she needed to find herself and I was so angry with her for leaving and not wanting to attempt to fix things right away that I pretty much threw her out of my life. But it had been three years already and this was the first I had heard of her whereabouts and I was going to bring my love home, no matter what.

As I went through airport security I felt myself getting a bit excited. By all counts, I knew this could be potentially dangerous, but Amity Crane wasn't a common name and she said she'd be going to Europe. I could only hope that she managed to get clean after she got there and didn't go to Amsterdam for the drugs.

I reasoned with myself that if I had gotten to this point, listening to a mystery man on the phone telling me where to find her, then I didn't really give a shit. I just wanted to bring Amity home once and for all so we could start over again.

An hour or so later, I boarded the plane, popped some Dramamine, and let myself drift off to sleep. I figured that if I slept for the whole flight, I'd wake up refreshed and ready to go.

Some hours later I was jostled gently awake by one of the flight attendants. She smiled at me and told me that we had arrived. I thanked her, got to my feet, and reached for my backpack that I had slid into the overhead compartment. Once it was securely on my back, I exited the plane and went into the terminal.

This was as far as I knew to go, other than this I felt completely lost. Part of me was expecting her to be waiting for me when I got off of the plane, part of me was wondering when I would realize this was a cruel joke.

But when I saw a pristinely dressed man holding up a sign that said Theo Lennox, I realized this might not be a joke after all. I walked up to him and showed him my ID to let him know who I was and he told me to follow him.

"First time in Amsterdam?" he asked, once I had gotten situated in the backseat of his car.

"Yeah."

"I hope you enjoy it then," he said with a nod as he pulled away from the curb and into traffic.

"Thanks. I'm just here to pick up my girl-friend honestly," I said, leaning back into the chair.

He glanced at me in the rearview mirror and nodded again. It was weird to me that I was so willing to go with this strange man that I didn't know, in a car that belonged to someone I didn't know, that I had put all of my faith in to get me to Amity.

Love will make you do crazy things, I thought to myself with a chuckle.

About forty five minutes into our drive we were in the heart of the city, only to be leaving it fifteen minutes later.

"Where are we going?" I asked him curiously.

"To your *girlfriend,*" he said, gritting his teeth on the last word.

"You know where she is?" I asked, leaning forward in excitement.

"In that house on the hill," he said using his index finger to point.

"I really appreciate this," I said, pulling the side zipper on my backpack open. I reached in and pulled out a twenty dollar bill, not knowing what it would exchange to in Euro, but figured that would be a nice tip for his driving me to where she was.

Ten more anxious minutes passed before we reached the house on the hill and he pulled slowly up the driveway before stopping the car in front of the door.

He got out to open my door and I handed him the money.

"Thanks. I didn't catch your name, by the way," I said, hoisting my backpack up my shoulder.

"My name is Kerstan," he replied with a small smile. "I appreciate the monetary gesture, but all the payment I will need is when you knock on that door and retrieve Lie—Amity," he said.

"She a friend of yours?" I asked curiously as I walked up the three small steps of the home.

"Something like that."

Hmm. I shrugged and knocked on the door waiting patiently. When there was no response, I knocked again and this time heard the sound of rushing footsteps coming toward the door.

It flung open violently and a man with an angry look on his face stepped out. I watched the familiar face as the anger gave way to shock.

"Smith?" I asked in disbelief.

"Theo?"

"And you'll find Amity inside. Now we're even," he said to my little brother, before he got into the car and drove away.

VICES
AND
VIRTUES

BLURB

In the Red Light District, you do what you have to in order to survive.

It's something I convinced myself of long ago.

Words that almost meant something once upon a time. But … the girls here in this house are treated so unfairly.

Punish all to punish one, and I don't know how much more I can take of this.

We can takes of this.

I've put up with the abuse for as long as I can, but while my friends are still here, I know I can't leave.

If we punish all to punish one, then I have to save us all to save myself.

I only hope I'll be strong enough to act when the time comes.

PROLOGUE

I WATCH them embracing each other, smiling and laughing, as the oldest of the pair holds the younger by the back of his neck. Their foreheads touch as they're happily holding onto each other; no words were further spoken after they said each other's names. Now they just stand there as brothers who hadn't seen in each other in years caught up in the moment of their reunion.

I knew I shouldn't be watching them because if Luuk caught me, he'd be so violently angry with me, but I couldn't help it. I had never seen an ounce of humanity in him until this man came to his door. But why? Why was he here? Is this what Ilse had put in motion? To have this man come?

I pulled my wild, thick brown hair back into a ponytail, securing it with a band that I had found in one of the girls' rooms. I pulled down on my loose gray tank top and reached down to smooth out my white shorts. Luuk allowed me clothes because I would just take them if he didn't and he knew it. My reflection in the mirror next to me caught my attention. I reached up and smoothed out the bumps on top of my hair and gave myself an encouraging nod.

Enter the room, sit down like you belong there and listen, I told myself.

I lifted my chin and brought up every ounce of courage I had inside of myself and walked past the two men, into the main sitting room where I knew they would eventually end up, and sat down in the largest lounge chair that belonged to Luuk. Bringing my legs up underneath myself, I leaned on the arm of the chair and turned my face toward them to wait. It worked as I knew it would. Luuk looked at me dangerously as he led the man into the room and they sat down opposite me.

"Hello," I greeted the stranger with a bright smile.

"Hi there," he replied warmly. "Is this your girlfriend?" he asked Luuk.

"Not really," I said before he had a chance to respond. "I mean I do all the things a good girlfriend would do, but I don't think we've picked a title for what *we* are yet, have we?"

On the inside, I was cheering. I felt like I had won a small victory because Luuk's face was crimson in anger and his lower lip was twitching. I watched him close his eyes for a moment, taking a deep breath to calm himself.

"This is my brother, Theo. Theo, this is Famke," he said gesturing between the two of us.

"Theo?" I asked in surprise. "Amity's Theo?"

I blurted it out and I knew I shouldn't have. It was just a shock I couldn't control and it made sense to me now why they had held each other so dearly. But would Luuk kill his own brother to keep his secret? Would he give him Amity Crane? Would he admit to everything he's put her through or even admit to what he had done to the rest of us?

"Yeah! Do you know her?" he asked eagerly. He leaned forward with wide excited eyes and I did my best to bite my tongue. If I blurted everything out he wouldn't believe me. No one's brother would do something like this to their love he would reason.

"I met her once," I said slowly. "In a café, near the Amstel River."

Theo looked at Luuk in shock before turning his attention back to me. "When? What was the name of it?"

An idea started to form inside of me. I would suggest something that Luuk couldn't say no to without having to explain to his brother.

"It's called *Singel 404*. I can show you where it was. It wasn't more than a week or so ago. She told me she frequents the place. If it's okay with Luuk that is," I said, letting my eyes drift toward him.

"Sure it is," Theo answered for him. I watched him get to his feet and drop his backpack onto the couch next to his brother. "Can you put this in a room for me somewhere? We'll be back soon."

A small smile crept across my lips as Luuk looked up at Theo. The look of absolute hopelessness in his eyes at what I could reveal about him outside of these walls ... about what he had done to Amity could destroy their relationship forever. And it was very apparent that they loved each other dearly, regardless of what happened.

"Perfect! Follow me," I said quickly getting up and extending an arm to Theo. "There's a lot about Amsterdam I want to tell you. Many, many things to see as well, but I promise we'll start at the café. We can wait for her there. I'm sure she'll show up."

I glanced at Luuk over my shoulder as I started to lead Theo out of the room. My eyes told him something that he I knew was worrying him. If Amity didn't appear later, I would tell Theo everything.

I WAS TRYING to keep my eyes open. It amazed me at how animated and spirited Theo was when Luuk himself, was cruel and curt with us. But the more he talked, the more I found myself coming close to nodding off and I had to keep an out for Amity.

Assuming she would show up that is.

I had a feeling she would, though. Luuk wouldn't be able to keep her hidden for too long, not when Kerstan had dropped his brother on his doorstep and told him she was there.

Don't get your hopes up, Famke, I told myself. *Luuk is a cunning, evil bastard.*

Another hour, three more cups of coffee between the two of us later, and I was ready to give up and just take him to Kerstan's home, when he suddenly stopped talking in mid-sentence.

I looked up from stirring my coffee and saw his eyes were trained on something behind me. Theo had tensed up so immensely that I was sure he would snap the handle off of his cup if he didn't put it down soon.

"What's wrong?" I asked, glancing over my shoulder.

For a moment I can honestly say I didn't believe what I was seeing. But when she smiled at us and Theo knocked his chair getting to his feet, I knew it was real.

Amity was crossing the street toward where we sat and she looked completely different. Her face showed no signs of the horrors she had faced in Luuk's home, the bruises on her arms were being hidden by some grand scheme on his behalf, and she walked with a confidence I had not seen since I found her alive in Kerstan's home.

Theo ran toward her and wrapped his arms

tightly around her. She laughed, put her head on his shoulder returning his hug, but looked at me with sad, pain filled eyes.

"I can't believe it," he said, finally pulling away from her. "My Ami." I watched him cradle her face in his hands as he kissed her gently at first, then kicked the passion up a notch.

I also watched as she struggled not to dig her nails into his forearms; a sign that any of us who worked in this district knew was indicative of an abusive House Master. Any form of touching makes you want to flinch, run away, save yourself.

When Theo pulled away from her again, she shot me a look that seemed to be begging for help, so I got up, dropped some money on the table and walked over. I put my arms around her waist from behind and picked her up in the air. It was a trick I had learn as a child when myself and whatever friends I had wanted a person we were interested in to give us some space. It caused the one being lifted to automatically lift their legs as a reflex and the person they wanted to move away to back up as an instinct.

"I'm so happy you came!" I exclaimed, turning her until she was behind me. Amity gave me a grateful smile and looked down at the ground.

"Smith told me you'd be here and that Theo wanted to see me," she replied softly.

"God, Ami, it's been so fucking long," Theo said, stepping toward Amity. I quickly stepped closer to him to keep the distance between the two of them, dismissing his frustrated look and took her by the hand.

"It's gonna have to be a little longer too, I'm afraid. Amity promised to take me shopping the next time we were both out together and this seems to be that time! We'll meet you back at the mansion," I said as I turned her around and started walking away from him.

"But—"

"No buts!" I called over my shoulder cheerfully. "We'll see you later!"

I squeezed Amity's hand reassuringly as we broke into a run down the streets of Amsterdam.

TWO

AMITY HADN'T SAID a word since the entire way to Amsterdam–Rhine Canal. I planned on taking her on a cruises to the Waal river since this was the first time we had both been out together. Once we arrived at our destination, I purchased two tickets and followed Amity onto the boat, settling next to her on the lower level.

"I never thought I'd see him again," she finally confessed quietly.

"How did it feel?" I asked gently.

She didn't answer right away. I glanced at her and watched her eyes searching the banks of the river, almost as if she were expecting an answer to appear.

"I don't know," she said with a sigh.

"You don't have to see him again if you don't want too. I can get a message to Kerstan and that'll be the end of that," I assured her.

A small smile danced across Amity's lips and I wondered if it was the thought of never seeing Theo again, or if because I had mentioned Kerstan's name.

"Do you miss him?" I asked curiously.

"I don't know," she repeated.

"No, not Theo," I said shaking my head. "Kerstan."

Amity got to her feet and walked to the metal bars that lined the outside of the boat. I watched as she leaned down and crossed her arms over the side. I stayed where I was seated, figuring she had enough people putting their hands on her lately, and crossed my right leg over my left. I would give her time to think about her answer, but it also lead me to believe that she *did* miss him in some way.

"Is it possible to miss someone who treated you so poorly? Who only saw you as a whore and sent you out more than the others because you made him the most money? Is it possible to miss someone who traded all of your friends away to make you feel alone? I wouldn't imagine it's possible to miss a man that groomed you to be the icing of the cake for another man's petty revenge. And yet ...," her voice trailed off.

"And yet, what?" I prompted.

"I think I do. I think I miss all of the bickering and the nights when he was kind to me. I think I miss the look in his eye when we shared private jokes. Whether I was his best and most used whore or not, Kerstan, even with his punishments, seemed to understand me more than anyone ever did," she finished wistfully.

"It's the House Master effect," I said with a nod.

Amity turned to look at me curiously. She crossed her arms over her chest and leaned back against the bars.

I smiled, "Basically it means that the Master of the House you live and work in, will do whatever he can to assure you the feeling of his love or whatever. He only reserves that for his favorite whore, because if she leaves, so does the money. I don't know, I could be wrong when it comes to you and Kerstan."

She turned her face away as she absorbed

what I had just explained to her. I honestly didn't know if it was different with Kerstan and Amity, but I didn't want her to suffer another unnecessary heartbreak, if that's all it was.

"You're probably right," she said, still keeping her gaze away from me. "I mean, if he really did feel something for me, he never

would've let me go to Smith's whorehouse."

"Something tells me he wouldn't have been able to stop you. Not if you're anything like me, because don't forget, I wound up on Kerstan's doorstep too after all," I replied mischievously.

She smiled and finally turned her attention back toward me. The smile on her face was pained and I could tell that I had struck the whore extraordinaire harder than Kerstan physically ever had.

I didn't know what to say in that moment. I wanted to apologize, but how many false apologies had she already received, that an authentic one would get lost in the shuffle?

We spent the rest of the boat ride in silence, Amity against the bars, me in the seats we had taken when we boarded. I felt terrible for most likely having shattered her perceptions of Kerstan, so I got up and went to the upper deck where the captain of the boat was and asked him to use a phone. After arguing with him for a few moments, I rolled my eyes, pulled the door closed behind him, and gave him a blow job in exchange for using the phone.

I dialed the operator and waited until she answered.

"I need to be connected to Kerstan .. Um.. Fuck. I don't know his last name, but he owns property on Reestraat street," I said to her in Dutch.

She told me to hold while she looked up the information. I tapped my foot impatiently until I heard a few clicks and was greeted by an old woman's voice.

"This is Famke. May I speak to Kerstan please?" I asked the grandmother. She told that she would get him if I didn't mind waiting. *Mind waiting? Some more? Why not?* I thought in aggravation.

"*Hallo?*" came the irritated voice.

"Is that how you greet a friend?" I asked, in a teasing voice.

"I'm not in the mood for games. What do you want?" he barked into the phone.

"What I want is for you to meet me on the

northern bank of the Waal river in half an hour. I'm on a boat right now and I'm sure that's how long it will take," I said, before disconnecting the call and tossing the phone back to the captain.

I jogged back down the steps and walked around to the side of the boat that I had been sitting on. Amity had turned herself back around to face the waters of the river and watch Amsterdam float lazily in front of us. Or was it us in front of Amsterdam? Either way, I felt like Kerstan would be able to circle the fucking city at least ten times before we docked.

Forty five painful minutes later, the boat finally began to pull into the marina, and I sprang to my feet. I walked quickly toward the edge that was facing the dock trying to get a glimpse of Kerstan. *If he even came.*

Finally deducing that he hadn't shown up after all, I waited for Amity so that we could walk onto the dock together. She had her arms still crossed firmly across her chest and I wanted to shake her and ask her when she had become this simpering girl that I was with all day. *That's not fair,* I scolded myself. She had been through more than the rest of us, physically, if not mentally. "Where are we going now?" she asked.

"I honestly don't know. I just wanted to put some distance between us and your past," I replied with a shrug.

"You're a good friend," she said softly.

"Am I a good friend as well?" we heard from behind us.

I turned around and laughed. I couldn't help it; somehow Kerstan had managed to work his way behind us in the crowd without being seen. It was my turn to cross my arms over my chest as I turned to look at Amity. She was looking at Kerstan with wide eyes, but at least her arms had dropped to her sides. I raised an eyebrow as they stood there and stared at each other wondering what was going through their heads, but when he stepped forward and took her face in his hands, it was safe to say that I figured it out.

He placed his forehead against hers and started whispering to her in Dutch how sorry he was that he hadn't told her what she was being bred for. He told her that taking Theo to Luuk was the only he knew he would be able to fix it; that if he saw what a devious bastard his brother had become, that she would be able to leave the Red Light District with her freedom. He promised her he would do whatever he could to prove his remorse to her, she just needed to tell him how.

In a way, I felt like I was watching an old French movie. There was obviously passion between them, but they knew they could never be and that the circumstances of what he had subjected her to would always pull them apart. Of course in those movies, they would end up together and live happily ever after, but how do you sell happily ever after to a girl that only knew how to sell herself?

Unless I give them a little push in the right direction.

THREE

Amity

KERSTAN APOLOGIZED to me more in those few moments on the dock than I had ever heard him do so in years to anyone else. The shitty thing was that I wanted desperately to believe him, but deep down, I knew I couldn't.

"You could've just let me go," I said back to him through grit teeth, tears starting to stream down my face. "You could've told me why you were doing this to me, Kerstan. But you didn't, so I don't think I can accept your apology."

"I don't expect that of you, Amity. I needed to say these things because they have been haunting me since you went to Luuk's home," he whispered back.

I pulled away from him and brought my arms back up over my chest. I could see Famke looking at us from the corner of her eye curiously. I knew what she was thinking; how was it possible for a pimp to possibly love one of his whores? If it was love that he was feeling anyway. I didn't know and I was entirely sure that I cared.

Having to deal with Kerstan possibly having these feelings for me and knowing that Theo still didn't make me feel any less used. It sure as fuck didn't make me feel any more human.

"How are my friends? How is Betje?" I asked him.

He sighed as he slid his hands into his pockets. The obvious rebuff of his feelings or whatever and he seemed to go back to the old bastard I knew. The one I could honestly say I actually liked.

"She's fine. She misses you," he replied, turning his attention toward the group of people walking past us to board the ship. "She tries to be like you; strong, charismatic, not caring. But I hear her crying sometimes at night in her room and I wonder why she thinks it's so bad to be in my home. I'm not as strict as the other owners and I give my girls more freedom."

"Freedom?" I scoffed. "You sell us to any man or woman willing to pay for the pleasure of our company, and you call that freedom?"

"Was I not kinder to you than Luuk?" he asked defensively.

"His name is Smith," I corrected through grit teeth. "And he's never been kind. Not since the day I first met him and not since the last day I saw him."

Kerstan sighed, his shoulders slumping as he gave Famke a hopeless look. She shrugged and crossed her arms over her chest. I knew she didn't want to get in the middle of what was happening with us, but I didn't want to let it go so easily. Only because, there *was* nothing between us. Even if I had felt something, the smallest speck of anything for Kerstan, it was gone the moment I discovered that he was grooming me for Smith.

It made me think of what Famke suffered in his house. What Wendeline went through and

Margit. What Valentina suffered to go back in and try to help me, though I still didn't really understand why.

"How's Margit?" I asked, glancing at Kerstan again. He shrugged in response; it was obvious that I hurt his feelings by not falling at his feet over his advances. "And Valentina?" Another shrug.

I was ready to grab him by his shoulders and shake it him back to sense; back to the smart ass, manipulative Kerstan that I knew, but I couldn't find myself to wound him any further. Not yet, anyway.

"You should take us back to your house," Famke suggested, brightly. "I'm sure the girls would love to see Amity!"

He nodded, kicking at the ground with the tip of his shiny black shoes and I sighed loudly.

"Kerstan, when are you going to be normal again? It hasn't been more than ten minutes and I'm already becoming aggravated by your little boy behavior."

I smirked when I saw that he was fighting a smile. The glimmer of the old Kerstan I knew was starting to shine dimly again in his eyes.

"Gimme a cigarette," I commanded, holding my hand out.

"What makes you think I have any?" he shot back with a raised eyebrow.

"Because if you *really* wanted to be in my good graces, you'd have a pack on you right now," I replied, my smirk widening into a grin.

Kerstan ran his hands through his hair, his eyes on me the entire time. My being a snappy bitch seemed to be working. I could see signs of "normal" Kerstan starting to creep across his demeanor. He was standing up straight again, with his shoulders back, and he had the usual cocky air about him.

I watched him fish around in his left pants pocket until he pulled out an unopen pack of my favorite brand of Dutch cigarettes, Cabellerro.

I took the burnt orange colored pack out of his hands happily and pulled the wrapper off of it. I put one between my teeth and held out my hand for a lighter which he quickly produced and used it to light my cigarette, inhaling deeply. I leaned my head back, eyes closed, and exhaled slowly.

"Careful, Janssen," I said, lowering my gaze

toward him, a grin spreading across my face. "I could get used to this."

"I wouldn't imagine that to be too terrible," he remarked with a laugh.

And to be honest, I didn't imagine it would be too terrible of a thing either.

Betje

KERSTAN HAD BEEN in a foul mood since he had come back from Luuk's. It was a bit of a blessing that he was gone for today. It allowed the rest of us to walk about the home freely and not have to worry about being sold for the day or night. All transactions went through him and if he were not here, there would be none to be had.

I spent most of my time with Valentina because she was the only one able to abide my newfound anger. After spending time as Luuk's personal play thing as well as being his "prized possession" I had become an entirely different person. The only one I could still say that I bore some semblance of love for was Amity, but even she seemed different. Broken almost, if I took what Famke and Valentina had told me to heart.

Even then, with Valentina being my closest friend since Amity had left, I still couldn't get her to tell me where Kerstan had gone too. He had seemed more nervous than I had ever seen him in ... Well I guess, ever. He had dressed in his best clothes before he left, making sure that not one hair was out of place, his shoes were shined, and smelled of a cologne I had never remembered in my time here.

I assumed he was going out to procure a trade and wanted to look his best. The nervousness was probably because he might be worried his foul mood would spill over into his business arrangement.

The longer I thought about it, the more I found myself not caring. The only business arrangement I cared about was how to get out of this life I had been sold into. Would I have to fuck ten more men? One hundred more?

No matter the number, I knew that Amity had

plans to fuck her way free of Kerstan's home and so did I. I would leave the Red Light District and I would go back to Germany. My family had probably given up all hope that I would ever be freed of this life, but I hadn't. I would go home and I would start a new life. I wouldn't worry about them because if they truly loved me, they never would have put me in this fucking place.

"You look angry," a voice remarked.

I glanced up from where I sat on Amity's bed and smiled grimly.

"Just thinking," I said to Valentina.

"About?" she prompted.

"Leaving this fucking place once and for all," I admitted.

"It *is* possible. But as far as I know, I am the only one who has been able to do it," she replied thoughtfully.

"How many?" I asked her curiously.

She smiled kindly, "More than I would care to admit to. Ever."

I sighed unhappily. I guess I should have kept count, but I had never thought of trying to leave until I had been traded to Luuk. He was cruel, unbearably cruel. His words stung harder than any hand he would lay upon us and there was a time where I thought that if I didn't get out of his house, I would kill myself.

In an odd turn of events, Kerstan actually rescued me from the house I so desperately wanted to leave but only through Amity's hand was I truly free from Luuk.

And now, I spend my days with Valentina as I said. I hadn't seen Amity since the day she told me that she would have to stay and that I would have to leave. I hated life without her, but I only hoped that she had followed in Valentina's footsteps and made her way to freedom.

"You think too much for someone that never asks for help," she added mysteriously.

"Help?" I asked in confusion.

Valentina sat down in the bed across from Amity's and crossed one leg over the other. She put her chin in her hand and looked at me for a moment before speaking.

"Do you know why I came back into this life? To help Amity. I had heard stories of her suffering and whispers of the plans against her. It touched me for some reason to think of this poor girl being set up the way she was and I wanted to do something about it. I wanted to get her out. It's not like it used to be when I first started. I wouldn't exactly say it was fun, but the House Masters were not like Kerstan and Luuk. They took better care of their girls, because they knew that keeping us happy, made us work harder."

I pulled my legs up and folded them underneath me on Amity's bed. Something told me that Valentina was thinking about helping us all, but she seemed to be more lost in her own thoughts of the past to worry about the present.

"So what do you suggest?" I asked casually, examining my fingernails.

"Do as I did. Earn your freedom," she replied simply.

"How?" I shouted. "Kerstan doesn't exactly keep count of how many men and women we've had to fuck!"

Her beautiful face melted into a warm smile. "There's something else about my leaving the Red Light District I haven't told you."

I stared at her, arms now crossed over my bare breasts, waiting for her answer.

"Bring a new girl in to take your place," she said, eyes widening, her voice barely above a whisper as she got to her feet and left me in the dorm alone.

Amity

FAMKE, Kerstan, and I walked around the streets of Amsterdam before he called for his car. He said we should go back to his home and figure out what the next step for me would be.

I exchanged a curious glance with Famke at his words, not sure what of the meaning. I decided to shrug it off though. Nothing Kerstan could say to me would erase the memories of the Red Light District. The countless number of men, women, and sometimes both at the same time, that I had satisfied to keep his wallet fat and his house standing.

I'd like to think that I was just as good as the Dutch girl, if not better, but was this really a title I wanted for the rest of my life? The best whore in the Red Light District wasn't exactly a title you would sit down and tell your grandchildren about.

I won't need to worry about that. I don't even know if I can have children at this point, I thought miserably, as I got comfortable in the backseat of Kerstan's car.

He sat beside me in the middle after pulling Famke out of the car. She attempted to sit between us and Kerstan was having none of it. When we were all seated and he gave his driver the go ahead, she leaned forward a little and gave me a questioning look. I crossed my arms over my chest giving her a slight nod, and turned my attention to the streets we drove passed.

Kerstan and Famke carried on a conversation in Dutch. I understood most of it and smiled because they both seemed to be forcing themselves to stay pleasant with the other.

There were moments in the long ride back, where Kerstan would lean closer to me and even resting his hand on my leg for a brief moment.

Nothing of which held meaning to me. I couldn't find comfort or genuine need from the touch of the man that had subjected me to so much. But I couldn't help wonder if it was worse than Theo's at this point. The touch of a man that still loved me, whose own *brother* was the reason for my suffering... Surely he must have known something about this, didn't he?

I decided not to think about it; not yet. It would put me in a foul mood full of paranoia and I'd probably try to jump into the Amsterdam–Rhine Canal just to escape the theories that would form in my head because of it.

Twenty minutes of spacing out to avoid the conversation and the ride later, and we were in front of Kerstan's house. I practically jumped out of the car before it came to a stop. I jogged up the stairs and pushed the door open without waiting for either of them. I wanted to see Wendeline and I wanted to see her now.

I walked through the doors smiling at some of the girls that had been here even before I got here. They were excited to see me and even though I was happy about it, none of them were her. I needed to make sure she was okay before I got my hopes up about Kerstan's plans.

"Lieve?" a voice said as I walked down the hallway.

I stopped in my tracks and turned around slowly. I knew the voice but the girl that stood before me was a shell of the one I knew and loved so much. Her eyes didn't hold light in them anymore. Her face looked so full of anger that I was almost afraid to approach her.

"Wendy?" I asked, softly.

The small German beauty ran toward me and threw her arms around my shoulders. She started to sob as I hugged her back and wondered what had been done to her to render her to what she now was.

"I missed you," I said, running my hands over her hair.

A loud sob was her response. She couldn't put her feelings into words, but I felt them through the trembling of her body. The tears that damp-ened my shoulder, and the way she held me against her.

"Well, that's a change."

I glanced up and saw Valentina standing in the doorway, a long red silk robe hanging loosely around her partially naked body. She was giving me a friendly smile, which I tightly returned.

He still keeps them half dressed, I thought in disgust.

"She was angry not a moment ago and now she's in tears. It's good that you've come back. I don't think she would've lasted much longer without you," she said, with a nod.

"Has she been mistreated since she's been back?" I asked quietly.

"No. Quite the opposite."

I raised an eyebrow to which Valentina responded with a laugh.

"Don't worry. He didn't take care of her the way he did you and me. He just made sure she didn't go out as often, and some days, not at all."

"I see Betje found you," Kerstan said from behind us.

She pulled away from me and wiped her eyes. I glanced down at her and gave her a small smile, before turning slightly toward him.

"Glad to know she's been treated well," I replied casually.

"I know this isn't what you wanted," he said, his face turning a little dark. "But it was the best I could do. I have a reputation to maintain."

I nodded, crossing my arms over my chest. I

was wondering where Margit was, but I didn't want to push him when his mood had shifted already. Walking into his whore house always turned him into ever the business man and I hated it.

Reaching into my pocket, I pulled out my pack of cigarettes. Before I pulled one out to light it, I pulled my shirt off and gave it to Wendeline. Kerstan scoffed as she pulled it over her head to cover herself and I smirked.

"This is still my place too, you know. I don't know if ownership ever officially changed hands, but I still like to think these are my girls to protect," I said, pulling out a cigarette and putting it between my lips. He rolled his eyes as he handed me his lighter. One drag as soon as it was on the flame and I handed it back to him.

"Speaking of which. How does one get out of this clusterfuck that I happen to be in?" I asked more to myself than him.

"Ask Valentina."

It was my turn to roll my eyes, punctuating it with a loud sigh as I turned my attention toward her.

"I don't want to play twenty questions. How do I do this?"

"What I did was not the usual way," she replied, looking uneasy for the first time.

"I love unusual. How did you do it?" I asked again.

"You fuck your way to freedom," she said with a shrug.

"Tell her the rest," Wendy commanded suddenly. "Tell her what you told me."

Valentina looked down for a moment, almost as if she were deciding if she should tell me or not. I took another pull on my cigarette, letting the smoke out in an impatient huff.

"*Valentina. How did you get out of here?*" I pressed.

"You have to bring another girl in to take your place," she finally said.

"No." I turned to face Kerstan again who had his hands in his pockets and was watching me with a bored expression on his face. "No way in hell am I trading another girl into this shit."

"Come speak to me," he said, turning on his heel and walking down the hall to the main dining hall.

"I'll be back, okay?" I said to Wendy as I walked passed her. She nodded, looking suddenly like a frightened child as I followed him.

Kerstan held the door open for me and when

I walked in, closed it firmly behind me. He gestured for me to have a seat, as he took his usual position at the head of the table.

"I'll make a deal with you."

I flicked the ashes on the floor and looked at him expectantly.

"I'm willing to forgive your debt, but I *do* want an exchange."

"It's not my fucking debt," I retorted.

"It became your fucking debt, when you entered my fucking house," he shot back. "Now stop interrupting and let me say what I have to say."

With another loud sigh, I sat back and listened to Kerstan's proposition.

Theo

I WASN'T sure how many hours had passed since I had last seen Amity, but I was sitting in my brother's house waiting for her to come back. I had to admit that I was a little uneasy here because there were so many people coming and going and a lot of the doors were locked, but he told me it was a boarding house, and Smith always was kind enough to do things to help other people.

"Will she be back soon?" I asked him for the

third time in half an hour.

"She should be," he replied with a laugh. "Her and Famke couldn't have gone far."

"Any idea why she did that? Walked away with her?" I asked.

"These boarders are a little odd. I mean they don't even call me by the right name sometimes. You've heard them," he replied with a shrug.

He has a point. That Luuk thing is weird.

"So, how long have you been living out here?" I asked him.

"Three years? I just wanted a change of scenery and to get away from that fuck up that happened," he said uneasily.

"Hey. I already forgave you for that, man. I forgave both of you," I reminded him, firmly shaking my head. "Shit happened. We're family; I'm not gonna hold it against you."

I watched the look of relief wash over my little brother's face and I smiled. I was glad that he felt better, because it was true. I forgave him; I forgave Amity too. I just wanted everything to go back to what it was before that night. Before everything went to shit. Before Amity left and Smith disappeared. Before I went into my fucking downward spiral of depression and constantly feeling alone.

I didn't want to be that guy anymore, and I refused to go back to America without my brother and the girl I wanted to marry.

Forty minutes of mindless chatter later, and I heard a familiar voice. "I'm back!"

I practically jumped out of my chair and went into the hallway. It was the Famke girl, but she didn't have Amity with her. The disappointment on my face must've been obvious, because her cheerful disposition faltered slightly.

"You okay?" she asked, raising an eyebrow.

"Where's Amity?"

"With Kerstan," she replied with a shrug.

"Who's that?" I asked in confusion.

"Ask your brother," she said with a small smile.

Frustration started to overwhelm me. It seemed like I had been doing nothing but playing a giant game of *Clue* since before I had arrived.

I walked back in the room I had been sitting in with Smith and threw myself into the seat. I was so annoyed by this point that I didn't want anything that wasn't a straight answer.

"Who's Kerstan?" I asked him evenly.

He looked at me for a moment, almost as if he were contemplating answering me.

"Who is he?" I prompted.

"He's the owner of one of the most prominent brothels in Amsterdam," he replied slowly.

"Brothel?"

"Yes. Amity works for him."

I sat back and stared at him in disbelief. If I had heard and processed what he said correctly, Amity Crane, the woman that I loved, was now a prostitute.

"What?"

My head was spinning. I felt like the world beneath my feet was trying to slip away and I was going to fall into the fires of desperation again. I had to have heard him wrong. I just had too.

"Amity isn't known by that name in Amsterdam," he said with a sigh. I closed my eyes tightly as he spoke and put a hand over them. I suddenly had the most terrible headache in the world. "Her name here is Lieve and she's the most prominent 'worker' in the Red Light District. From what I understand, she takes enough clients to make Kerstan a very rich man."

Just then, Famke entered the room and sat down on the couch across from both of us. She

275

quickly examined her fingernails before turning her attention to our conversation.

"Did you tell him?" she asked.

"Yes," Smith replied tightly.

"All of it?" she asked.

"I told him what matters," he snapped at her.

She scoffed and crossed her arms over her chest, turning her face away. I let my gaze go from her to my brother and back again, before I realized that she knew more than he was telling me.

"Give us a minute," I said to him.

"For what?"

"Just give us a minute!" I shouted.

Smith had always been stubborn. Even when we were children, so him refusing to move out of his seat came no surprise to me. I'm sure it didn't come as any surprise to him either, when I grabbed him by his arm and pretty much tossed him out of the room.

I sank back down in the chair I had been sitting in and looked at Famke. She smiled at me with knowledge beaming in her eyes and I nodded.

"The truth. All of it. Please," I said, leaning forward.

"Amity is known as Lieve in the Red Light

District. She got trapped her because of some shitty debt that a family in Italy she was staying with owed. That's how it usually happens here. You owe a debt, you fuck it off by working in someone's home. With Amity, there was always gossip that the family never really owed a debt and that this was personal. But when she ended up in Kerstan's home, we were all kind of surprised. We all knew that they didn't know each other; it was obvious by the way he treated her at first. A lot of us thought she ended up in the wrong house, but after a while, the truth came to light and what a bitter truth it was. Your precious baby brother hired Kerstan to use Amity as revenge for whatever happened between them in America. I heard him one night talking to Kerstan on the phone, telling him that if he worked her harder than the other girls and made sure she was used the most, that you would never take her back. Not the way she would be returned to you. I honestly don't think he ever meant to return her though. I think the reason you're here is because Kerstan developed some kind of feelings for Amity and he wanted you to see what your brother had done. It's a pretty vicious cycle, if you ask me," she finished with a shrug.

I got to my feet and started pacing. I don't know why I thought it would help, but I was shaking at this point and I need to start moving to offset the feeling. This person who I had just met and had no reason to lie to me whatsoever, was telling me that my brother arranged for my girl-friend to become a whore in someone else's brothel to make sure that I wouldn't take her back.

"I'm willing to help you get her out of here, but there's a few things I want in return," she said quietly.

SEVEN

Betje

I WAS SITTING on Amity's bed again, while Valentina sat behind me brushing my hair. She told me I reminded her of a doll she had when she was a child and her favorite past time was brushing the doll's hair. I didn't mind it; if I was able to provide a simple solace for someone in this never ending Hell, then I would.

"What do you think they've been talking about for so long?" I asked her, nervously chewing on my thumb nail.

"He's probably telling her he'll let her leave *if,*" she said emphasizing the last word.

"If?" I echoed curiously.

"Where do you think I got the idea from bringing in a girl to replace me?" she asked in a clipped tone.

Of course. That would only make sense. She never seemed like a bad person.

"Sorry," I replied quietly.

"It's okay," she said with a sigh. Valentina moved the brush away from my hair and shifted herself on the bed behind me. "I guess it's why I felt bad for Lieve. If a debt is honestly owed, then there's nothing to be done, but work it off. That wasn't the case with her and when I heard the rumors, I thought maybe I could trade myself back into this so she could get out."

"Why would you want to come back to this?" I asked her in disbelief .

"I don't. But she'll never find someone in time."

"In time for what?"

Valentina got up from the bed and left the room. She obviously knew way more than she was saying and I was starting to feel nervous.

In time for what? I thought to myself. I had to find Amity and find out what she spoke about with Kerstan. I had to warn her that there wasn't enough time. I didn't know how I would explain what it was supposed to mean, but I would tell her that the warning itself came from Valentina and I would find a way to get her as far away from the Red Light District as I could.

As I left the room, I couldn't help but feel a flicker of sadness inside of me. I didn't know how much money I had made and if Kerstan would even allow me any to gain passage for Amity. If he didn't, I would had to sneak her out in the middle of the night somehow.

I walked quietly down the hallway, my arms wrapped around myself toward the door of the main dining hall. I can see the door as I approach, now cracked slightly open and found myself wondering if they were even inside of it.

I stopped short in front of the doors and took a deep breath, before I looked in through the sliver of space.

I let my breath out when I saw Amity seated in her chair, legs spread open, and Kerstan kneeled before her.

The look of pure ecstasy on her face gave a clear indication of what was happening. I stood there hidden behind the doors watching as he pulled back and slid his fingers inside of her. Her body was somewhat rigid with desire as he moved his fingers quickly before replacing them with his mouth again. She reached a hand down and firmly gripped a handful of his hair as she arched her back as she started to moan.

The sounds that came from her were controlled; almost as if she were trying to fight her own desire but couldn't under his skillful hands and tongue.

"Kerstan..." she gasped as her body stiffened once last time, before more moans escaped her and she fell back against the chair in satisfaction.

She ran a hand back through her hair as he rested back onto his heels, his hands on her thighs. He said something to her I couldn't quite make out but she smiled and smacked his hands away.

Amity got to her feet and pulled her shorts and panties back on, pulled Kerstan to his feet, and shoved him into the chair. He fell back with a laugh and watched her as she unzipped his pants.

I rolled my eyes.

If this is what they were "talking" about so

privately then perhaps she had made her mind up to stay with him.

I turned my eyes away for a moment to glance behind me at the sound of footsteps, but when I was satisfied that the footsteps were not coming toward me, I turned my attention back to Amity and Kerstan, only to find his head now resting comfortably back against the head of the chair and Amity on *her* knees, her head moving up and down.

Slow then quick, slow then quick. Kerstan not as able to keep his moans as quiet as Amity was echoing off the walls in the room.

I sighed and left my position by the door only to run into

Valentina who was watching me with curious eyes.

"What are you doing?" she asked.

"Lower your voice!" I replied frantically, pulling her down the hall. "They're *busy* and I didn't want them to catch me watching."

"They're fucking?" she asked in disbelief.

"No. Well on their way, though," I replied dryly.

"Then now is my chance," she said, straightening her robe around her. "Go back to your room. We'll come for you when this is over."

By this point, I was so sick of Valentina and her riddles that I did as I was told. I decided in that moment that if Amity truly wanted to leave or wanted my help, she would either do it on her own or ask.

EIGHT

Valentina

I PUSHED OPEN the doors to the dining hall slowly, deliberately. I wanted them to know I was there, but without just bursting in. It would disrupt the mood and I couldn't have that. Not with what I was intending at the end of this.

Kerstan opened his eyes with a gasp. Amity stopped sucking his cock long enough to turn around and see who had entered the room. A smile crept across my face.

"Mind if I join?" I asked them, undoing my robe and letting it fall to the floor.

Without waiting for a reply, I went over to Amity, placed a hand on her shoulder, and dropped to my knees next to her. I took Kerstan's throbbing cock from her hand and began to stroke it, pressing my lips against hers.

Our kiss was deep and passionate, something I knew I would never feel again after tonight. It wasn't the passion that I thought of it was the feeling of desire. I had been used so many times by so many men and women, that genuine desire was something that was lost to me.

I pulled away from her lips, only a breath and whispered, "Leave when I engage him. This will be the only chance you have."

She looked at me in confusion at first, then in understanding, and with a slight nod, moved her hand to cover mine on Kerstan's cock. Together, we began to stroke him until he reached his climax, spilling his cum all over our hands.

"Go," I whispered as I got to my feet, hand still firmly on his cock, and slid it inside of me as I sat down on his lap.

I never thought I would have to fuck him again. Even though he was the most skilled man I had ever been with, the thought of having him inside of me again was something that still brought back haunting memories. The ones I had fought so hard to push back into the darkest corners of my mind came back with each movement of my hips. But when I heard Amity's footsteps retreating quickly from the room, I considered it a small victory and kept Kerstan pinned to the chair as I fucked him to climax again.

His body shuddered and his breathing became quick as he sat there, his hands on my hips, trying to regain his sense.

"I know why you did this," he finally said, his eyes closed.

"And you didn't try to stop me?" I asked curiously.

"No."

"Why?" I asked, moving his hands away from me and getting shakily to my feet.

"Because we've already come to an agreement, she and I," he said, reaching for one of the cloth napkins on the table and cleaning himself off. "What you just did was pointless, but well received."

"Then why the fuck did you let me do it?" I

asked angrily, going to retrieve my robe and wrap it tightly around myself.

"Because I was in the mood and you interrupted. It was the least you could do," he said getting to his feet. "Go to Luuk's. Bring him and his brother and Famke back here. This is going to all end tonight," he commanded as he walked past me and left me standing in alone in the room.

I WAITED until the sun was descending over the horizon before I set out to Luuk's house. Kerstan had said it would end "tonight" so I wanted to keep his words literal. The cab took me to the end of his driveway and I walked up it confidently. I didn't know what Amity and Kerstan had planned, but for me to bring back such important people in her wrongdoing and salvation told me that I was going to enjoy whatever happened.

The steady hum of the engine of the cab as it waited for my return soothed what little nerves I had. Luuk wouldn't be able to do anything to me without it being witnessed and the police alerted.

When I reached the door, I knocked loudly and kept doing so until Luuk pulled the door open clearly irritated at the sound. "What do you want?" he asked through narrowed eyes.

"Kerstan and Amity request your presence. As well as your brother and Famke," I said loud enough for the entire house to hear, before promptly turning on my heel and practically running down the driveway.

NINE

Famke

WE SAT QUIETLY, piled into the back of Luuk's car, as his driver took us to Kerstan's house. I wasn't sure what the urgency was but when Theo heard Amity's name shouted he grabbed his coat and walked out the door. In a way I felt sad for him; it was almost as if though he still hoped that everything would be forgotten and they could go back to the way it was before.

Luuk's deception and his plans to make her into a used whore unworthy of his brother failed miserably and I promised him that I would do my best to get them back together. All I wanted in return was freedom from this place, his brother to pay to what he did to us, and a home to all my own. Everything to which he readily agreed to.

I hope they're as easily agreeable as he is, I thought to myself as I watched the city go by from the backseat. I was so ready for this to be over and to have a normal life again. I would be sad that the other girls would have to find a new house to work for, but I needed this so much. I needed normality and I needed to be on my own for a while. It was the only way I'd be able to start to heal from this mess.

Twenty minutes later, the car stopped and the doors opened. His driver had opened mine and gave me a friendly smiled when I stepped out. I turned my attention to Theo who was walking straight toward the door in sheer determination.

I raised an eyebrow, wondering why he was so eager to be rejected. I knew Amity wouldn't want to leave with him, but I thought that if I could secure everything else and give him a glimmer of hope, I might be able to get what I wanted.

The door swung open before he had a chance to knock and I smiled at the grandmother. It was obvious that she had been anticipating our arrival. Theo walked right past her without so much as a glance and I apologized to her when I approached. She shook her head to let me know it was okay and let her eyes flicker slightly up and to the right. Before I stepped into the house, I saw Amity watching us from an upstairs window. When our eyes met, she smiled and disappeared from view.

"They await you in the main dining room," she said to us in Dutch. I motioned for Luuk to follow me and called out to Theo for his attention.

"This way."

They fell into step behind me as we entered the room to find Kerstan sitting at the far end, Betje and Valentina on either side. Amity walked in after we had taken our seats at the opposite end of the table and stood behind Kerstan, her arms crossed over her chest.

"What is this about?" Luuk barked.

"A deal," she said with a smile starting to dance across her lips. "Kerstan releases me of my debt and he's letting me take Wendy with me," she said putting a hand on Betje's shoulder. The small German girl looked up at her with wide, surprised eyes, before bursting into tears.

"At what cost?" Luuk asked, leaning forward curiously.

"Simple. I had to find someone to take my place and I did," she said, her smile widening.

"What the hell is going on? I just want to leave and for you to come with me," Theo said in a strained voice.

Amity turned her attention toward him. The smile left her face, and her eyes became serious. She looked like she was carefully thinking of her words before she spoke them.

"I don't love you anymore, Theo," she said softly. "Your brother, what he had done to me, what he did to me *himself*, it turned me bitter against the Lennox family. I won't be able to look into your eyes without thinking of the Red Light District. I won't be able to stomach your touch without thinking of *him*. I'm sorry that you came all this way for nothing, but I'm not going back with you. I can't."

With as much as I didn't want to in that moment, I turned my eyes toward Theo. He sat there with such a desperately hurt look on his face, that I realized I was finally witnessing what heartbreak actually looked like.

He put his face in his hand and pulled away

from his brother's grip who was trying to apologize to him for everything he had done. I don't think his words of trying to atone would hold much worth with Theo now.

"Don't hate me just yet. I haven't told you the true price of my freedom. The person I've chosen to take my place will probably cause the both of you as much shame as I was caused, but there's no way around bargaining it. In the time since Valentina went to fetch the three of you, the plan was already put into play and she'll be leaving America in the morning," Amity continued, regaining her air of composure.

"Don't you fucking dare," Smith warned, getting slowly to his feet. It was almost as if he knew what we're happening and the rest of us who weren't Amity and Kerstan were still stumbling around in the dark.

"She'll do just fine here. She'll finish working off the hell you wanted to put me through. Another five or so years, we figured," Amity said with a smirk. "A beautiful young girl, with golden brown hair and eyes to match. Pale of skin, and slender will fetch good prices in any house she's placed in. Which brings me to the other part of this. Kerstan, in the morning, will bring the

House Masters together to remove you from yours and any power you hold as one in Amsterdam. Your house will be passed to Famke and Kerstan's to Valentina. You're fucking done in this country, Smith. You're going to be left with piss and shit, and that's all you deserve."

"You can't do this," Smith shouted, slamming his fist against the table.

"It's already being set in motion. You're in *my* house and you will watch your tone or you will be escorted out into the cold where you belong. We kindly offer you one more night in your house to get your affairs in order. That's all you will receive," Kerstan said with a smirk.

"Nicola will be here in the morning like I said. By that time, the two of you will be gone and if you're not, don't think you'll be able to get to her since we've already got an all-day client for her. Wendy, go get your things. Valentina, Kerstan will sign his house over to you in the morning. Famke, the same will go for you with Luuk."

"What about the two of you?" I asked, curiously. Kerstan glanced me and grinned.

"I have more than enough money to go wherever I please. I perhaps will come visit you once in a while, as well as Valentina, but I think I'll just go to the only place I've always wanted to see. America."

"And you?" I asked Amity.

"I never did finish my adventure in Camogli. I think I'll go back to the beginning and go from there," she said with a big smile, as she grabbed Wendeline by the hand and lead her out of the room.

EPILOGUE

2 Years Later

MY NEXT ADVENTURE, I decided would be to Germany. I hadn't seen Wendy since we had left Amsterdam and I missed her. I wanted to catch up on things and see how she had been adjusting to life outside of the Red Light District.

I had received a postcard from Valentina and another from Famke last week, which was the usual when it came to them. It was how we kept in touch; a few paragraphs on a small piece of cardboard paper to let the other know we were still alive and doing well. It was usually that way with Wendy too, but I hadn't gotten one from her in the past few months and that was when I decided it was time to go see her.

When the plane landed in Berlin and I waited patiently in line to exit, I wondered if she would still look the same. I had gone back to my blonde hair, I was starting to feel a bit like the old Amity too. I knew it would take a long time to be me again, but for now, I was slowly working my way toward it.

Five minutes later, I exited the plane and found a spot in the terminal where I could put my backpack down. I crouched onto the carpeted floor and unzipped the front pocket to fish out the last postcard I had received from her. I peered at her address again before walking out of the terminal and got into the waiting cabs line.

I kept the postcard in my hand, because my German was rusty and I figured if I just showed the address to the driver, it would be easier than struggling to pronounce it.

Ten minutes later it was my turn and I happily got into the backseat, placed my backpack onto the empty spot next to me, and leaned cross the divider to show him the address. He nodded and pulled away from the curb when the moment presented itself.

I smiled at all of the small shops and how different everything looked here. Almost everything I saw reminded me of her when I first met her. Small, unassuming, and full of wonder.

I was hoping she'd be excited to see me. I knew that it would probably bring back painful memories, but I wouldn't feel better about not hearing from her if I didn't know she was at least doing okay.

Half an hour later, the cab pulled up in front of a small brick apartment building and before exiting, I handed him fifty American dollars. He glanced at it curiously and I waved my hand to let him know that I wasn't worried about change or anything. With a happy smile, he waited until I removed my backpack and closed the back door before he drove away.

I looked down at the post card again to find the apartment number, before I opened the door and walked into the building. I went took the stairs to the second floor and walked past all of the doors glancing at the numbers to see if I had found hers yet, when I was greeted by a familiar face.

"What are you doing here?" I asked in excitement.

Kerstan looked up and dropped the box he was holding. He came over to me and wrapped his arms around me, holding me tightly against him.

"It lifts the heart to see you," he whispered into my ear as I returned his tight hug.

"Is that Wendy's place that you just walked out of?" I asked curiously, pulling away from him. "Yes."

"What's wrong?" I asked, noticing the solemn look in his eyes. "And what's in the box?"

"The last of her belongings. I was going to take them to her parents since they can't bring themselves to come here since she died."

"What?"

I felt like the world was starting to spin beneath my feet and leaned against the wall to hold myself up.

"Didn't you know?" he asked quietly. "Wendeline hung herself here a few months ago. She left a note saying that she would never be herself again and it ate at her every day. She said that she wanted her family to have her things, but she wanted you to have this," he said, reaching down and pulling a small rectangular item off the top of the box.

I looked down, tears glazing my eyes and saw Wendy's smiling face sitting next on my favorite iron bench in Kerstan's garden. My legs were propped up on her lap, a cigarette in my hand, and pulling a face.

"They removed this from her body. She had it pinned to her shirt along with the note."

I sank down to the ground, held the picture tightly against my chest, and cried uncontrollably. It would seem that even though I was starting to get myself back on track, the Red Light District had scarred some of us deeper than others.

Some of us would never be able to let the feelings of being unworthy and used let go. Some of us weren't as strong as I thought we could be.

It was my fault for not getting her out sooner. I knew it was; and because of that I would go back to Amerstdam. I would go back with Kerstan and I would force him to let me finish what I had started.

He would agree to it. I knew he would.

After all, I was his best girl.

About Yolanda Olson

Yolanda Olson is a USA Today Bestselling and award-winning author. Born and raised in Bridgeport, CT where she currently resides, she usually spends her time watching her favorite channel, Investigation Discovery. Occasionally, she takes a break to write books and test the limits of her mind. Also an avid horror movie fan, she likes to incorporate dark elements into the majority of her books.

View Yolanda's books by scanning here:

FREE BOOK

Grab your FREE copy of What Lies Beneath by
scanning here:

*"The atmosphere is dark and ominous, and there's
seemingly no escape from the monster. But the question is,
who is the real monster?"*
– USA Today Bestselling Author Ellie Midwood

Milton Keynes UK
Ingram Content Group UK Ltd.
UKHW022343020823
426203UK00017B/743

9 798988 483816